JACK HAWKE

in *Killer Game*

MICHAEL LANCASHIRE

In memory of Terry Pratchett,
whose books brought me immense joy
as a youngster, and who I find myself
quoting more and more often as an adult.

JOIN THE **JACK HAWKE FAN CLUB** AND BE
ONE OF THE FIRST TO HEAR WHEN A NEW
JACK HAWKE BOOK IS RELEASED

Sign up now and get a FREE copy of the 12 page
reports that *TOP SECRET* spy agency CIRCLE pulled
together on their newest teenage spy.

I promise I'll never spam you, but you'll get things like:
behind the scenes information on Jack, exclusive free
stories, updates, book release details and more. I
will never pass on your email address and you can opt-
out at any time.

YOU CAN SIGN UP AT
www.sannox.org.uk/jack-hawke-sign-up/

CHAPTER ONE

"You need to see this. The police sent it over."

The well-dressed man in the expensive suit burst into his boss's office and waved his tablet computer at her.

His boss looked up at him, annoyed by the interruption, but she sat silently as he moved his fingers over the tablet in a fast sequence of taps. She was a thin woman, sharp and pointy as though if you got too close to her you might cut yourself. And she had a personality to match.

A second later he finished and his tablet screen was copied onto the big monitor in front of her.

They watched it together.

"Who is this?"

"His name's Paul Jefferson. He worked for Morton Tech."

"Work-*ed*. Past tense?"

"Keep watching." The man's eyes never left the screen, but out of the corner of his eye he saw his boss raise an eyebrow and quickly remembered his manners. "I'm sorry, I mean keep watching, *ma'am*," he added.

He had worked for the sharp-looking woman for some time now but even he didn't like to get her angry. When she got angry then she got very polite and bad things happened.

"What's he doing?" she asked.

"He seems to be trying to arrange them in some sort of order, ma'am."

"An order. An order of cereal boxes?"

"And tins of beans and soup, yes."

"Right."

She kept watching. As strange as it sounded that was exactly what the man on the screen was doing. Stacking boxes and tins, then taking them down and rearranging them.

"Could it be some sort of message?" she tried again.

"Perhaps. It looks to me like he's trying to solve some sort of puzzle."

"Hm," she agreed.

"This is it, any minute now."

The man on the screen stood and walked out of the shop. The video jumped to a shot from a different camera, this one outside the shop. It showed the same man as he walked across the pavement. He paused for a second on the edge of the pavement. Further down the road a speeding lorry came closer.

When it was about five feet away, the man on the screen stepped calmly in front of it.

The well-dressed man looked at his boss.

Her face showed no emotion but her voice was a little quieter as she asked, "Is he...?"

"I'm afraid so, ma'am."

Both of them were silent for a moment, giving him some respect. Then the man spoke again.

"We've been able to keep it quiet but I think we have a problem. This is the third. They're never the same, but all just as strange."

"He said something before he killed himself. What was it?"

The man kicked himself. He hadn't spotted it, but then his boss's eyes were as sharp as the rest of her. He rewound the recording until the moment just before Paul Jefferson stepped into traffic.

"What's that he's mouthing," the woman asked. "Pawn? Is it some sort of chess thing?"

The man peered closely at the screen, rewinding it and watching the horrible moment for a third time.

"No, he's saying 're-spawn'."

"Oh." She nodded. "What does that mean then?"

"I have no idea, ma'am."

CHAPTER TWO

Jack Hawke sat up straighter in his chair when the door opened and his brother walked in. He flicked his hand in a small wave and tried to smile.

The smile that Bobby Hawke flashed back at him had no sign of concern on it. It was his usual big smile that showed all of his teeth in his round face. The wave he tried to go with it wasn't quite as successful.

He tried to raise his hands but could only get them as high as his chest. The handcuffs shackling them to his waist wouldn't let him lift them any higher. He looked down as though he was surprised and shrugged.

Jack sighed and waited for the prison guards to escort his brother to the chair opposite him.

Jack was fourteen. Prisons weren't a good place for fourteen year olds to be. Still, he supposed it was better to be sitting on this side of the table. That was what he was here to talk to Bobby about.

Bobby took his seat and grinned again at his little brother.

"What's up little man? You look miserable," he said as the guard stepped away from the table.

"I need to talk to you, Bob."

His brother frowned ever so slightly for the first time since he'd been brought into the room. He'd picked up on the serious tone of Jack's voice.

"Go on then."

Jack took a deep breath. He knew his brother wasn't going to like this, but there was no easy way to say it.

"I'm going to tell them it was me."

Bobby shook his head furiously.

"You are not," he said with a finality like a door slamming.

Jack raised his hand in a calming motion and carried on.

"Hear me out Bob. I'm much younger than you. They're going to try you as an adult and you'll end up in here for years. If I tell them it was me, I'll be treated like a kid." He hesitated. "Besides... it was my fault."

Bobby looked around, terrified that someone would overhear. He lowered his voice.

"Don't say that. Don't ever say that. It wasn't your fault. I chose to break in to that warehouse, not you." They both knew that wasn't completely true. Bobby had got caught but they had both been there that night. And the plan had been entirely Jack's. He'd chosen the target, a designer jeans warehouse; he'd worked out how to disable the alarms and the security cameras; he'd been the lookout. He'd planned the whole thing down to the last minute for Bobby.

"I spoke to your solicitor. She says that if you give up who you were working with they'll go easier on you."

"You didn't tell her it was you, did you?"

I wanted to but I chickened out, he thought. "No, no. I just..."

Bobby's shoulders sagged with relief.

"Good, they want me to roll over on B14. They don't think I did it on my own but they don't think it was you.

They reckon the rest of the gang were involved and they want me to give them a list of names. If you tell them it was you they'll just throw away the key on us both. They won't need me any more."

B14 were a street gang that Bobby ran with. They hadn't been involved in the warehouse job at all. It wasn't really their style. They weren't saints but they were more into dealing soft drugs to the local neighbourhood. They certainly didn't go in for complicated plans like the one Jack had come up with. Jack had planned to use them afterwards to fence some of the designer gear they stole, but when B14 stole stuff themselves it was usually just a smash and grab.

Jack didn't know what to do. He had come here with a great speech planned that was supposed to save his brother from the mess they had got into, but what Bobby was saying made perfect sense.

"But you're not going to roll over on them are you?"

"No."

"So you're going to end up in here for a long time." Jack tried to ignore the lump he could feel forming in his throat. "Bobby, this place... Can you... How will you handle it?" In truth he didn't suspect his brother would last in prison. When they'd been growing up Bobby had been the tough one, but this was different.

Bobby grinned at him again.

"Hey! Hawke's don't give up man," Bobby said. It was one of his favourite sayings, he'd said it every time one of them had anything difficult to deal with over the years. And growing up in different care homes they'd had plenty of difficult things. It had become a running gag.

The trouble was that the last thing Jack needed right now was Bobby being funny. He struggled not to cry.

His brother saw it in his face and reached forward over the table to comfort him. At the same time the handcuffs stopped him and the guard was up off the wall and pushing towards them. Bobby snapped his hands back quickly and showed his palms to the guard in a surrender pose. The guard was satisfied and went back to leaning against the wall.

"Look Jack, I appreciate what you're trying to do but it won't help. Besides, you have too much ahead of you to waste it in here. You've always been the one with the brains. Use them to get out of this life, not further into it."

"If I was that clever the plan would have worked right?" Jack snorted. He hadn't told Bobby, but his whole plan had been designed to get them out of this life.

"Don't be soft. It was a good plan. It just didn't work. You couldn't have known that security guard would come back looking for his wallet. Anyway, that's enough about this. Tell me about you. Where are you staying?"

"They've moved me to a new foster home."

"Any good?"

"We've had worse. They're alright really. There's eleven kids though, so you don't get a lot of attention."

"That a good thing?" Bobby knew his brother well.

Jack smiled. "Yeah, it is."

"Any trouble from the other kids?"

"None. It's like I'm not there."

"Perfect, right?"

"Yeah. Perfect," Jack said and hoped that Bobby believed him. He had always felt happier on his own but with Bobby in here he felt alone for the first time. They'd always been there for each other. "Ty said he'd look after me."

Ty was the leader of B14. Bobby shook his head uncertainly.

"I'm not sure it's a good idea for you to be around B14 at the moment Jack. Maybe steer clear of them until this settles down, hey?"

"Why?"

"Because if you get caught up with them it'll finish your life. You'll always owe them something. And I don't want that for you, I want you get away from all of this. Make a better life for yourself."

"You mean for us, right?"

"Yeah. For us." Bobby said awkwardly. "You go straight now and make it big, then when I get out of here I'll come and scrounge off you. Deal?"

Jack laughed. "Yeah, deal."

Jack stood and awkwardly extended his hand to shake Bobby's, glancing nervously at the guard to check he was allowed. The guard nodded once and Bobby reached up as far as the handcuffs would let him. Jack shook his brother's hand and then turned and walked away as quickly as possible.

His head was in a mess as he walked to the door.

He had no clue what to think.

He knew he was clever, cleverer than any of the children he had come into contact with in his life so far, and most of the adults too, but he'd never known a life that was different from the one he and Bobby had grown up in.

Could he do what Bobby wanted? Could he make it in the straight world?

The sharp-faced woman and the well-dressed man stood watching Jack and Bobby through the one way mirror.

"Will he go for it?" the man asked.

"I don't intend to give him a choice. He's perfect for what we have in mind. I've reviewed the job they say his brother did. There's no way he came up with it. It was him." She pointed at Jack.

"Are you sure? He's only a kid."

"A kid who planned a fairly complicated theft and got away with it."

"He only got away with it because his brother took the fall."

"And his brother only got caught because a security guard was in there when he shouldn't have been. It was a good plan but plans sometimes go wrong. Any of our best agents could have had the same thing happen in the field. You know that. I've read his teachers' reports and his tests show amazing results. He has an IQ of 144."

"What about his brother? Maybe he's smart too and it really was him."

"Him?! I'm not sure he could even spell IQ. No, it was Jack."

The man nodded, she was right of course. She usually was. But he was still concerned.

"Okay, but brains aren't everything. Do we want a kid who's already prepared to break the law at his age?"

"Oh come on, Wallace! All of our people have to break the law at some point. Besides, think about the theft itself. He planned just about as victimless a crime as he could get. Stealing ridiculously expensive jeans from a company that can easily afford it and doing it without anybody getting hurt. If one of our agents came up with the same plan you'd be impressed."

The well-dressed man, whose name was obviously Wallace, agreed but sometimes his job was to challenge her. Carefully, of course.

"Hm. I read those same reports you did though and every one of his teachers said he's a troublemaker. No one has been able to control him."

"They haven't had the right lever to pull. We have." She nodded her head towards Bobby.

"Well, you're the boss." The man adjusted his pocket square and watched as Jack thrust his hand out towards his brother to say goodbye. "Do you think he'll be able to pull it off?"

"I don't know. But we might as well try. We don't have any other options for getting in there and anyway..." She shrugged carelessly.

"He's expendable." He finished the thought for her.

"Exactly. He has no ties to us and if it goes wrong then, like you said, he's just a kid. Even better than that, this is a kid no-one cares about."

CHAPTER THREE

That evening Jack was sitting glued to a monitor playing SWAT Team IV. It was Jack's favourite escape from the rubbish that was his normal life. In truth he was a bit obsessed with it.

He was in the back of a little shop that unlocked mobile phones and did computer repairs. He worked at the shop after school a couple of times a week on the till so that the owner, Frank, could concentrate on solving whatever tech problem someone had brought him. He wasn't working today, but Jack and Frank got on really well so Frank let him hang out there even when he wasn't working.

Frank was twenty-something (Jack had never asked exactly how old he was) and a proper geek. And he loved SWAT Team IV too. He had wider gaming tastes but still enjoyed the game enough to play it every day, and that was good enough for Jack.

The arrangement was ideal for Jack because it meant he could stay away longer from whatever foster home he had been dumped in and, most importantly, it gave him somewhere to keep his gaming PC. He had built it from the parts of four old ones that were brought to Frank but were broken beyond repair. If he'd kept it at any of the foster homes one of the other kids would have stolen it or broken it.

SWAT Team IV was a first-person shooter in which you controlled an operator on a police armed response or SWAT team. One of the things Jack loved about it the most was that it had different game modes. The basic mode was an open world so you could send your character anywhere you wanted in the game world and do anything. It was like exploring. You never knew what you'd find. But it also had a mode people used for competition where you had to complete specific missions, or maps. Depending on the mission you might have to storm a building and rescue a hostage or simply find and kill all of the enemy team.

Jack liked the competitive missions best.

He had built a team of players that he played with regularly and he even hoped to play professionally in the pro-leagues when he was older. Bobby didn't get it. At the moment the big teams were all from America but there was a growing European scene that Jack, under the username Jaybom, was a part of. He supposed it was easier in America where there were millions of people all speaking the same language. In Europe the language barriers meant that most teams were nationally based so they drew from a smaller pool and didn't have the same opportunity to find talent.

Jack thought he had found a way around that. His team all tried to speak English but he enjoyed learning other languages (although there was no way he was letting his teachers know that) so he'd set himself the task of speaking to each of them in their own language. It meant they could all react quicker. His French, Spanish and Italian were all pretty much fluent and he could get by in German. He'd even learnt a bit of Flemish last year to speak to one lad who had been on their team for a short time. He hadn't lasted long though, and Jack's efforts to learn Flemish had stopped with him.

His team weren't pro-league yet but he reckoned with another year or so of practice they might get picked up by one of the smaller organisations.

It was weird really, he had never met any of them but they were the closest thing to friends he had. He wasn't unpopular at school. In fact there were lots of people who'd probably think of him as a mate, but he had never really felt a solid connection with any of them, never found a particular group he bonded with. B14 definitely weren't his real friends, he knew that. If they were anyone's friends at all, which he doubted, then they were Bobby's. He was just someone's kid brother. With his SWAT Team IV team on the other hand, and even the wider SWAT Team IV community, it was different. They shared an obsession. And he could be himself.

"Tolka, a la droite!" he screamed into his headset, warning his French teammate of the shooter on his right.

The teams started with five operators in but there was only him and Tolka left alive right now.

Tolka spun but she missed her shot and the player from the other team got her first. Jack ran over to see if he could restore her health but it was too late, the other player had got her in the head and there was no coming back after that. If this was a casual game she could respawn somewhere else and all she would lose would be the time it took her to get back to the action. But this was a game that counted towards their rank so there was no respawning.

It was all down to Jack now. 1 v 1. The rest of his team were all locked out of the game until it finished. That made it exciting but he wasn't worried, he had done it before plenty of times. Maybe he sat up a little straighter in his chair.

For some reason the player who had shot Tolka had stayed in full view but hadn't taken the chance to shoot at

Jack, so Jack ducked his operator behind a burnt-out car and tried to take him out, but the other player just stood up and ran off. He was running away from the main building, presumably hoping to time Jack out. Now it was down to the two of them a new timer had started, and if he didn't finish off the other player in three minutes then his team would lose. He'd have to track him down and kill him.

Jack ran after him, turning the corner of the building and guessed that he'd have to sprint to the outfield. That was where most people went to time out the attackers.

What was that?

He brought his character to a stop.

That was odd. He knew the game and all of the maps like the back of his hand, but he had never seen graffiti on this wall before.

He spun his operator around quickly to be sure that the other player wasn't hiding somewhere to take a shot at him. The area was fairly open, though, and there was no sight of him so he guessed that he had rounded the next corner and was still heading towards the outfield. Jack crouched his operator down so that he was less likely to be seen and turned to get a good look at the wall.

It wasn't actually graffiti after all. A sign had been added to the wall with crude letters on it. It said:

Wait here J

'J'? Was this supposed to be a message for him?

The sign had definitely never been there before and he knew for a fact that there hadn't been a new release of the game.

Still scanning the area to make sure the other player didn't sneak up on him, Jack pulled one of his headphones away from his ear and called loudly to Frank.

"Frank, have you seen anything weird in the game today?" There was no need to spell out which game.

"Weird?" Frank called back from the front of the shop. "Like what? No, nothing weird. Well, there was this one

guy, I think he was German, he was a complete spanner..."
Frank went on about the player he had been teamed up
with that morning but Jack tuned him out. Whatever it was
it couldn't be relevant. If Frank had seen a sign like this
he'd have known what Jack meant by 'weird'.

He pushed his headphone back into place and focused
on the game.

Whatever this was it would have to wait. Someone was
probably just messing about. He'd heard about hackers
messing with games before, he'd just never seen it on
SWAT Team IV. And the J was probably a coincidence. It
was probably the handle of whatever hacker had done it.
He only had two minutes left to catch this guy and kill him
before he lost the game. He turned away from the wall
intending to chase him down.

As soon as he did two things happened: the other player
stepped into view and, at precisely the same time, a message
landed in his in-game chat function. Nobody but noobs
used the chat function so it distracted him enough that he
glanced at it before taking a shot at the other player.

What it said was weirder still.

>Jaybom do not shoot. Please follow me

The character walked away.
Jack froze, unsure of what to do in the game or the real
world.

Three seconds later, when Jack hadn't moved, the
character came back around the corner and took another
couple of steps towards him.

>Jaybom I need your assistance, please come with me.

What should he do? He typed out a quick "Who are
you?" and tried to send it to the other player but it wouldn't
go. The game showed the other operator as a non-player

character. That meant there wasn't supposed to be a human player behind it, the computer was controlling it so you couldn't send it messages. But whoever was controlling that operator had sent one to him. Jack's eyes flicked back to the main screen area. And then he properly freaked out.

The operator had come closer and was now holding a sign like the one on the wall, but this one read:

Jack Hawke. Follow character. Now.

Jack jumped up so fast it knocked his chair over and then reached forward and punched the power button to turn off his machine. Then he started pacing around the room.

None of this should be possible.

Someone had written on the wall when it wasn't supposed to be possible to change the in-game graphics unless you worked for the manufacturer.

And they had communicated through a non-player character.

And most frightening of all, they knew his name. His *real* name.

Maybe, just maybe, referring to you in-game by your handle was a clever new feature that the manufacturer was releasing, but there was no way anyone in-game knew his real name. Even the manufacturer. Sure you had to register with them but he was too young to play SWAT Team IV legally so he had registered his account under a fake name.

He stared at the blank screen.

What is going on?

Well, there was really only one way to find out.

He stood his seat back up from where it had fallen over and sat down before gingerly turning the machine back on. He had to find out who was behind that operator.

Jack rebooted his machine and let it run a diagnostic to make sure he hadn't done any damage by turning it off without closing it down properly first.

Should I call Frank to watch? he thought. *No, I need to make sure it happens again first otherwise I'll look like a real spoon.*

Frank wouldn't take the mickey out of him but he didn't want him thinking he was an idiot.

The diagnostic finished and confirmed that the machine was still fine so he fired up SWAT Team IV and waited impatiently while it ran through the opening credits. Once it was ready he selected the same map he had been playing before. He figured the best chance of seeing the message again was to do exactly the same as he'd done last time.

He chose the same operator, the same weapons, even the same charms he had used to decorate his in-game gun and set off to follow the same path as before.

He ignored the questions that were coming in from his teammates and selected a game with random players. He'd have to explain to them what had happened but he didn't have time now. Besides, they were all used to being called away for things like meals at the most inconvenient times so they'd understand.

He ignored the gameplay around him and concentrated on staying alive to make his way to the same spot outside the building as last time.

He didn't know whether to hope the signs were there or not. It was cool but it was freaky.

As he turned the corner of the building he realised he was holding his breath and let it out.

Sure enough, the signs were still on the wall and the message was still on the signs.

Wait here J.

This time though the mystery player was nowhere to be seen so he did as the sign said and waited.

He waited for a whole minute.

Nothing.

He checked the game counter, he had come straight here this time so it was quicker. Maybe whatever had happened was triggered by the clock in the game.

He waited some more.

He couldn't be sure how much time had elapsed last time but he knew roughly how long his usual play on this map took and he would have been here by now. This was stupid.

Twice another player approached and tried to kill him. Twice he defended the position and returned to stand by the wall. Still nothing. He gave up, he obviously hadn't imagined the signs but it looked like the other player wasn't going to show.

Screw this, he thought. *I might as well get on with the game.*

He turned his operator away from the wall.

"Holy crap!" he shouted in real life.

The same operator from last time was standing right behind him and for some reason he hadn't heard him approach. That shouldn't have been possible either, the game always let you hear footsteps. Presumably it was another symptom of whatever hacking was making this work.

"You alright?" Frank called through.

"Oh! Yes, yes, I'm fine, just got a great headshot, tell you later."

The character was holding the same sign as last time.

Jack Hawke. Follow character. Now.

Okay, Jack thought. *I will but how do I tell you that?* He couldn't send a chat message while the game thought this person was a non-player character and he certainly couldn't make his own sign so he had no way to communicate. He just stood there and hoped whoever it was would work out that he was on board because he hadn't tried to shoot them. Or freaked out and turned off his computer.

After a second the operator started walking away slowly and Jack followed. After four steps he stopped and turned to check that Jack was following, seeing that he was he picked up the pace and led the way away from the building, away from the area with the other players in to reduce the chance of getting shot and having to re-spawn.

Eventually they arrived at a little building outside of the main farmhouse that the players called 'Outhouse' and the operator went inside. Everyone who knew what they were doing on SWAT Team IV ignored Outhouse because it couldn't be used in any good strategies, but whoever was in charge of this operator must have some plan so Jack followed.

As soon as they were inside Jack did another double take. Having led him all the way here the operator simply disappeared as though the player had turned off their computer and dropped out of the game.

Now what? But his question was answered as soon as he focused on the room he had been left in.

"Holy. Crap..." he said again slowly, separating the words with a nod of his head and letting out a low whistle.

The inside of Outbuilding had been decorated with signs like the one the character had been holding. Obviously whoever had done this had worked out the code for that one hack and was using it to do everything they needed. Whatever that was.

The walls were totally covered and the way the signs worked you had to look directly at them to be able to read the writing, so where to start? He spun his character around and saw the none too subtle clue. One of the signs had a large arrow on it. He moved his character over to the sign next to it and started reading.

The message was broken into a number of different signs that filled the walls, but in such a small building and with writing big enough to be seen the final message was actually quite short:

Jack Hawke. We know who

you are and what you did.

If you want to

Protect Bobby

Meet us in

Highbury Park

At 09:15 tomorrow

Come alone.

CHAPTER FOUR

The next morning Jack sat alone on a bench in Highbury Park seriously wondering if he had gone mad.

This is stupid, what am I doing here?

He knew all the advice about online security. How you should never meet anybody in real life that you only knew from the internet, how people online could pretend to be anyone. But this was different, they *hadn't* pretended to be anyone. If someone was trying to trap him into something then surely they wouldn't have tried to be so mysterious.

Maybe the whole thing is a hoax. But no, they knew his name. Nobody should be able to know his name and tie it to his in-game username. And they knew something about Bobby. However weird it was he needed to find out what was going on.

Should I just go back to the home?

He glanced at his watch. 9:14. There was still one minute to go until they were supposed to meet, but surely if it was real they'd be here by now.

No, he came to a decision. This was dangerous. He was leaving. He'd go to Frank's place, log back on to the game and demand to know who was at the other end of it before he would meet them.

He placed his hands on the bench and pushed himself up.

"Jack Hawke, I presume," came a polite voice from behind him.

Jack jumped and spun around, shocked by how close the voice sounded. He tried to hide his fright and looked the man in front of him up and down. He was wearing a dark blue suit and waistcoat. He looked more like some sort of high-powered lawyer than a hacker who could have broken in to SWAT Team IV.

Jack pushed down his nerves and tried to sound as grown-up and in control as possible as he replied.

"Yes. And you are?"

The man smiled. He was obviously aiming for friendly but it came off as patronising.

"One of the people you are expecting to meet. We sent you a message last night."

Well, thought Jack. *He certainly sounds like he knows what he's talking about and I'm pretty sure child abductors don't wear waistcoats to the park.* But he wasn't an idiot and he wanted to be sure.

"How do I know it's really you? Tell me what the message said."

"We told you we knew about Bobby. We sent it through a game."

"What game?"

The man looked momentarily blank then scrunched his face up and took a stab.

"SWAT something?" he said uncertainly.

Jack shook his head in despair. It always amazed him how something that was such a large part of his life could be almost unknown outside of his normal circles. But he guessed it was as much proof as he was going to get.

"Okay then, what do you want?"

"First off, take this." The man handed Jack a white stick which he had taken from an inside pocket and unfolded.

Jack took it automatically and asked, "What is this?"

"It's part of your disguise. We are going to our headquarters but for now you can't know where they are. And I can't escort you through the park blindfolded, can I? So I need you to put these on."

He handed Jack a pair of dark glasses with wide plastic edges along the side. Jack took them from him and looked at them.

"You want me to pretend to be blind?"

A smirk flashed across the man's face but he got control quickly. "Not pretend," he said. "I want you to put these on and become blind."

Jack looked at the man questioningly, should he really do this? Maybe he should just refuse and leave now. He hadn't told anybody he was coming here. If anything happened to him then nobody would know for hours.

But then, he thought sadly, *who would I have told anyway?*

The man in the suit saw the hesitation in Jack's face and nodded understandingly.

"I get it, Jack, it's weird. But you don't have a lot of options here." The man's eyes darted around the park and he decided to take a chance. "I can't tell you much out here but I will tell you this: we need your help and you can trust me when I tell you that we are the good guys."

Jack shrugged. He didn't like trusting anyone but the man seemed honest enough, and he had got this far so backing out now seemed pointless.

"Alright then," he said and slipped the glasses on. The world went dark and he held his arm out. "I assume you are planning to lead me?"

"That's the idea."

The man took his arm and started walking.

The man led Jack to a waiting car. As they went he kept up a constant stream of commentary on where Jack should put his feet and anything he needed to be careful of. Jack guessed the idea was to give him the reassurance of human contact rather than the actual information.

When they reached the car Jack heard him open a door and then felt a hand on the back of his shoulders. He guided Jack into the back seat so that he did not bang his head on the door.

The man got into the driver's seat and as soon as his door had shut Jack reached up and touched his glasses.

"Can I take these off now?" he asked.

"No!" the man said quickly. "They need to stay on until I tell you otherwise."

Jack dropped his hands into his lap and the man said nothing more. A couple of seconds later Jack felt the car start.

At first Jack strained to hear anything that might give him a clue as to where they were. He had seen films where the hero was kept in the boot of a car and was able to identify which direction they had gone in from the bumps in the road and the muffled sounds, but it was hopeless. He could tell they were alone but the windows of the car were shut and the sounds that did make it through gave him no clue where they were going.

Even the time would be no use. He had read a Sherlock Holmes story when he was younger where a man was driven for a couple of hours only to discover he had been driven in circles. He could be anywhere.

He supposed if he knew the exact amount of time they spent driving then it would be possible to put a maximum perimeter on the area they could have got to. But this was

Birmingham. An area a couple of miles square would have literally thousands of buildings in. He would stand no chance of finding it again unless they wanted him to.

He gave up and did his best to relax. It didn't work.

After about fifteen minutes Jack felt the car stop, and heard the engine turn off and the man get out. He opened Jack's door and took Jack's arm gently.

"This way. Mind your head again," he said.

Jack got out of the car and the man guided him forwards. For the first time Jack's hearing was actually able to tell something useful about the outside world. One minute there was the rush of traffic and the next it was muffled and an echo sprang up from their footsteps.

He smiled as he realised that he could tell they had walked into a narrow alleyway.

He barely had time to be pleased with his new-found ability, though, before the man brought him to a stop and spoke quietly.

"You can take the glasses off now but keep looking forwards. I really don't want you trying to work out where we are. Understood?"

"I understand," said Jack reaching up to take off the glasses as quickly as possible. He did as the man said and resisted the urge to turn around and look behind him.

He had been right about being in an alleyway. What he'd been unable to tell was that it was a dead-end. They were standing right in front of four big metal rubbish bins. They were the sort that shops used but they didn't have anything on that would have helped Jack work out where they were.

"So, is this it?" Jack asked. "Is this where I get to find out what's going on?"

"In a minute," the man said and stepped forward to one of the bins.

He rubbed some dirt off the big 'O' on the logo of the bin's manufacturer and Jack wondered what on earth he was doing. Then it got weirder. The man leant forward and pressed his face close to the bin as though he were smelling it.

That's nice, Jack started to think. *Doesn't really fit with your posh clothes...* but then his inner monologue crashed to a halt and his eyebrows shot up.

The centre of the 'O' opened up like the iris of a camera and a red beam shot out.

The man held his face still and the beam scanned his eye. It must have liked what it saw because a second later the bin split down the middle and the two halves swung open.

Jack could see past the man to the inside of the bin but it was nothing like any bin he had ever seen before. Inside it was a room with crystal clean white walls and floor.

The man stepped inside confidently.

"You coming?" he asked Jack who was standing there with his mouth open.

The white room turned out to be a lift.

No sooner had Jack stepped inside it than the man in the fancy suit looked up at a camera on the ceiling and nodded. The doors swung shut and cut them off from the alleyway behind them.

Jack was about to ask a question when the man raised a finger to silence him.

"Agent Wallace plus one guest," he said in a flat monotone.

Well now I know his name, but 'agent'?! thought Jack. *What have I got mixed up in here?* This guy didn't behave like the police and anyway they were always moaning about not having enough money. Secret entrances and laser beams must cost a lot. If Jack had to guess he'd say he was a spy.

He tried to think what he could have done that would have attracted the attention of people like that but he couldn't think of anything. There was no way the warehouse theft should bring down spies on him.

A red beam like the one outside swept the room and a small beep went off. Jack just about had time to wonder what it meant when the room started to drop.

Jack's stomach lurched and he wobbled slightly on his feet.

Agent Wallace stretched his hand out and took Jack's shoulder to steady him. Jack was grateful but he just nodded. He didn't want to be overly polite to the man who had basically kidnapped him.

"So what is this place?" he asked as the lift powered down at amazing speed into the ground underneath the city.

"You'll see."

Eventually the lift came to a halt and the doors opened onto a very different scene from the alley above. Jack looked out in amazement. Almost everything was pure white, the walls, the ceilings, the floor, most of the furniture.

Jack had been in a number of hospitals over the years, usually for reasons he'd rather not remember. Although people thought of them as white the reality was they were almost always painted a variety of shades of 'dull'. Sometimes the dull was brown, sometimes it was grey, sometimes someone tried to liven it up a bit and used an actual colour like blue. But always the dull managed to seep through like they'd used it as an undercoat.

This was what they had been trying to achieve. It was like a hospital from the future. The white screamed 'clean' at you.

"Follow me," Wallace said and walked briskly off without waiting to see whether Jack did or not.

Jack stepped out of the lift and his feet clanged loudly. He looked down and his stomach lurched for the second time that morning. The walkway was made of a metal grating like they used in prisons and Jack could see straight through it. His head swam and he stepped quickly forward to grab hold of the railing in front of him. It didn't help. Now that he could see over the railing it was worse. He could see more than just the brilliant white colour that had overwhelmed him at first. The whole place was built around a huge hole in the ground. From where he was he could count five levels beneath him but he had no way of knowing if that was as far down as it went. He couldn't see the bottom of the hole at all.

Once the feeling of vertigo had passed and his brain had kicked back in properly he thought it looked pretty cool. Because of the central pit everything was curved. It looked as though a giant had punched a hole in the ground and whoever had built this place had just built around the outside in a ring, then built another ring on top of it and kept going adding more rings whenever they needed more space.

It reminded him of a rocket launch site or a lighthouse.

"Are you coming?!" Wallace called back, still walking away.

He pushed himself off the rail and scurried to catch up with Wallace, his steps crashing against the metal walkway as he ran. He fell into place next to Wallace and walked alongside him.

His mind boggled as they passed doors with names like 'Weapons Development', 'Telemetry' and 'Poisons'. He had a thousand questions to ask but since Wallace hadn't told him anything so far he decided to keep them to himself.

Wallace stopped when they reached a door that said simply 'Director'.

"This is us," he said and waited outside it without knocking.

Evidently whoever was inside was expecting them because the little intercom on the right buzzed into life with a crackle of static.

"Come in Wallace," the voice said and there was a clunk as the locks withdrew and then the door opened automatically with a hiss.

Wallace gestured with his head for Jack to follow and then led the way in.

CHAPTER FIVE

The room they stepped into looked completely out of keeping with the rest of the place. It belonged in a castle or a Victorian gentlemen's club. The few walls that weren't covered with bookcases were covered instead with oak panelling. The rug on the floor was a deep green and must have been an antique.

And the desk, wow, thought Jack, *the desk.* It was huge and old. Very old. It looked like it had been built by the same carpenter who made King Arthur's round table, but this time the instructions hadn't included anything about making people feel equal.

While the rest of the building screamed modern, hi-tech and professional, this room was all about power. And it didn't shout at all, it whispered very quietly how powerful it was. How powerful it had always been. And how powerful it would always be. It murmured that it was immortal. Whoever occupied this office would have power for as long as they lived and, when they died, they would be replaced by another person who would be equally powerful. The only boast the room made was that the specific people would come and go with their tiny short lives but the office would last forever. Powerful.

Jack felt small. In a strange way it was similar to the feeling of vertigo he'd had a moment ago.

A woman's voice snapped Jack out of the spell the room had cast and brought him back to reality.

"Jack, forgive the odd way we brought you here but we needed to be sure that nobody knew."

He turned to see where the voice had come from and saw a woman standing at what looked like a window. She turned as she spoke but she had been standing with her hands clasped behind her back looking down through the window as though they were high up above the ground.

Now that is cool, he thought when he realised it couldn't possibly be a real window. The scene was incredibly realistic but if it had been real then it would have looked out onto rock.

Jack stopped thinking about the window and focused on the woman herself. She reminded him of an eagle. Her features all seemed to come to points and he could easily imagine her swooping down and grasping him with her beak or talons. She obviously belonged behind the desk. She gave off power in almost the same way the room did.

"Why am I here?" he said bluntly, refusing to be cowed or to play along with their polite game. Jack didn't like power. The people in his life so far who had power tended to be the sort of people who shouldn't have it. Anyway, they had all but abducted him and they all knew it. There was no way he was going to be all nicey-nicey now.

"Ah, straight to the point. Fair enough. I'm not much given to messing about myself either. Take a seat."

Jack thought about objecting but decided there would be no point. He sat down and the woman did likewise, slipping comfortably behind the big desk. It should have dwarfed her but somehow she fitted into it perfectly.

"So...?" he was going to keep being blunt until they explained what was going on.

The woman's eyes narrowed a fraction and Jack saw that his refusal to play their polite game was irritating her, but she ploughed on as though it wasn't.

"I imagine you're wondering how we got the message to you," she said calmly.

It annoyed Jack that she was rising above his sarcastic comments so he decided to be less subtle.

"I'm wondering why you're not getting to the point," he said and rolled his eyes openly.

For a split second the woman's mask dropped. Jack saw the icy reality beneath it and regretted provoking her.

"Let. Me. Be. Clear," she said, each word dropping like a guillotine. "I am not one of your teachers that you can back-chat with impunity. Irritating me could have severe consequences for you. And your brother. Luckily for you I have a degree of patience and, despite your best efforts, you are not annoying me. Yet. But you would do well to remember that you are a child, Jack. When I was your age children learnt manners."

Jack bit back the smart comment that popped into his head and instead tried for a nonchalant shrug. It didn't quite come off as carefree as he would have liked because in truth he was a little scared of her. The whole situation was weird and this room and its owner were the icing on the cake. His earlier fears in the park about being abducted by some sort of child molester were obviously wrong, but they had been replaced by something even more worrying. And it was still true that nobody knew where he was. This office would think nothing of crushing little people like him. It had probably done exactly that for centuries.

"Very well," the woman continued. "Since you have no interest in small talk let's get to it. This place is the headquarters of a government department called CIRCLE."

"I've never heard of you," Jack said but he was careful to sound polite this time.

"You wouldn't have. MI6 and MI5 are the only British intelligence agencies most people know about. A very few people might also have heard of the Joint Intelligence Committee. All of those groups solve different types of problem for the UK government. But when *they* have a problem, they come to us. CIRCLE is the oldest and most secret British intelligence agency."

"So you're the head spies?"

"We don't like to talk of it that way. But yes." Looking at her behind that desk Jack could believe it. "Anyway, something has come to our attention that we... I... want your help with. So listen very carefully, your input will be required."

Jack's eyebrows raised, what could they possibly want his help with? But he sat up straighter and paid attention.

"Do you know of Morton Technology?" she asked.

"They're supposed to be bringing out some sort of new game at GamesCon. It's called Shark but no-one knows what it is. They've been doing some teaser ads on SWAT Team IV, never says anything about it, just 'Shark is coming' in that movie trailer voice." Jack imitated the voice.

The woman looked slightly nonplussed. "Well, that's as maybe but more importantly they're also a contractor for the Ministry of Defence. They work on some pretty dangerous, top secret stuff."

"Oh, right." Jack felt silly focusing on gaming when everything here was obviously a lot more serious but the woman had moved on regardless.

"There have been three odd deaths in the last four weeks involving employees of Morton Tech. The first was a man who committed suicide by police. Do you know what that is?"

I'm 14 not 4, Jack thought but again he had the good sense to keep it to himself.

"Yes," he said instead. "It's when someone does something illegal and then gets himself shot on purpose. Happens a lot in America."

"Well a month ago it happened here too. Or so the coroner believes. A man stole a car and got into a high speed chase with police before apparently losing control and crashing into the side of a railway bridge. The coroner concluded that the driver had done it with the intention of getting killed."

"I saw that on the news. Wasn't it just a car theft gone wrong, why do they think he wanted to die?"

"Once he'd stolen the car he waited at the entrance to the motorway for the police and media to catch up with him. Only when they were ready did he speed off and later crash. It looks like the chase was the point."

"Oh."

She nodded.

"And then there was Kate Edwards. She was involved in a horse riding accident."

"That doesn't sound particularly odd."

"She rode the horse off a cliff," she said and Jack's eyes widened. "Have you ever ridden a horse, Jack?"

"No."

"It's been ruled accidental death but it's not easy to make a horse run off a cliff. They're not cars. She must have worked very hard to do it. Then there was this. Wallace."

At a gesture from his boss Agent Wallace turned off the lights and a screen lowered from the ceiling. As it slid into place the video of the man in the supermarket started to play.

Jack watched curiously. The man on the screen's behaviour was undeniably odd. The ending made Jack wince but he he'd had a fairly tough life so he didn't look away.

When the screen retracted and the lights came back up Jack saw that both the sharp-edged director and Wallace were looking expectantly at him. They were obviously waiting for some sort of comment but he didn't know what they wanted from him.

"Okay I'm guessing you think they were all murdered. But what I don't get is that, if you think that, then why are you looking into it and not the police?"

"As I mentioned at the start Jack, Morton Tech are a defence contractor so if somebody is trying to kill their employees then this is potentially a matter of national security. We need to establish what's going on there quietly."

"It could be a coincidence."

Wallace snorted but the woman nodded.

"It could," she said. "In fact I hope it is. But in my line of work it doesn't really pay to believe in coincidences. Anyway, better to be safe than sorry."

Jack nodded thoughtfully, she was probably right. Then he asked the most important question.

"Alright, say I agree, there's probably something going on there. What has any of it got to do with me? You said it yourself earlier, I'm just a child."

"Ah, that's just the thing, Jack. You're perfect for what I've got in mind!"

Here it comes, Jack thought. *People with power always have an agenda.*

"We need to know what's going on in Morton Tech," the Director continued. "And like you said, Jack, they are releasing this Shark game soon and, whatever it is, they want it to be a big thing. They ran a competition to get volunteers to join a testing team on their site and half of them are children from schools. We want you to go in there and take a look around then give us a report on what's going on."

"You want me to spy on them?"

She hesitated slightly then nodded. "Yes."

"But it isn't like it is in the movies, Jack," Wallace said from the chair beside him. "Spy work is boring. All you'll be doing is a bit of sneaking around. Maybe leave one or two listening devices..."

"Bugs?"

"Yes, bugs. Leave one or two bugs in some places you can get to. Nothing dramatic."

Jack didn't like it. It was one thing to fantasise about being a spy it was quite another for it to become real.

"I don't know," he said uncertainly. "If they're a defence company then they work for the government. Why don't you just go to whoever is in charge and tell them what you're worried about?"

"That's not how we work," Wallace said. "We keep things quiet."

"We don't know what's going on or even how high up their company it goes," the Director said and then shook her head as though the decision was made. "No, the testing competition is perfect. There's no connection between the game and the deaths but it gives us an excuse to get you in there. We've arranged for one of the existing testers to become ill and need to go home. When she does you're going to go in as her replacement."

Jack shifted in his chair. He decided not to think about how they'd 'arranged' for this other tester to become ill. But the Director was speaking as though this was all agreed, as though he had no say over it, and he couldn't let that go.

"Hang on a minute," he said as politely as he could, deciding after the last time that there was nothing to be gained by angering her unnecessarily. "I'm grateful for you asking me but I haven't said I'll do it yet."

"No. But you're going to." The Director raised her eyebrows and clasped her hands on her desk in front of her. Jack tried to speak but she cut him off. "Jack, please believe me I am doing my best to keep this civil. There are lots of good reasons for you to do this. You're bright, you're observant and you're a gamer so you'll fit in perfectly. And, as we've both agreed, you're a child so if anything is going on there, then whoever is behind it won't ever suspect that you're looking into them. I meant it when I said you were perfect for this. If I were you I would leave it there and do a service for your country." She stood up and leant across the desk. "But if none of that is enough for you to do the right thing, just cast your mind back to the message that brought you in here. We know you were involved in Bobby's break-in and I will have no hesitation in telling the police that. Now think about where you are, Jack, and believe me when I tell you that we have a certain amount of influence over your brother's sentence. Breaking and entering could give him quite a lengthy time in jail couldn't it? Of course, if you've been helpful to the government, well... things might be different."

Jack sat frozen in his seat. He couldn't believe what he was hearing.

"That's blackmail," he said.

"Let's call it an incentive. You still have a choice. But I suspect you're going to do exactly as we want because the consequences of the other choice aren't very pleasant. For you or Bobby."

Jack sat silently for thirty seconds. They obviously needed him or they wouldn't be putting so much pressure on him. And if they needed him then maybe it was an opportunity to help Bobby.

"If I do this I want you to get Bobby released. Not on remand, not tagged or anything. Released."

"We..." Wallace started to speak but the Director interrupted him.

"Done," she said.

"Just like that?" Jack asked.

"Just like that. I don't care about your brother's crime, Jack. A petty warehouse theft means nothing on the level we play at. Find out what's going on here and the government will be very grateful."

Jack nodded, eager to believe her.

"Okay, I'm in. What do we do now?"

CHAPTER SIX

At the same time as Jack was being press-ganged by the Director of CIRCLE, another well-dressed man (though this one was more casual than Agent Wallace) was pacing backwards and forwards angrily in front of a big videoconference screen, wearing a path in the expensive, thick carpet of his top floor penthouse suite.

Simon Morton, the owner of Morton Tech, was having his usual meeting with his heads of department. Apart from Morton's executive assistant, Marcus Sauer, the rest of them were downstairs in the Boardroom at their usual seats around his board table. Simon had his own similarly grand table but, since he had jumped up and was storming around the room, it seemed lost in the massive space of his penthouse with only his skeletally thin executive assistant sitting at it.

"I still don't understand what the hell he was doing in a supermarket unattended! Can someone explain to me how that happened?" Morton demanded. There was a pause while the others all looked at each other. Nobody wanted to be the first to speak and draw attention to themselves. "Anyone!"

When it was obvious that nobody else would speak, a woman in a white lab coat answered.

"We don't understand either, sir. He must have reacted badly to the protocol. That's not unusual, as you know, but then he wandered off. I've spoken to security and they've looked at the video from our cameras. When he left here he seemed perfectly normal, he had a breakdown outside."

Morton had nowhere to go with that. He couldn't very well hold his people responsible if the man had shown no signs at all.

"Well, I want everyone involved in the testing to be super careful from now on. We cannot afford to draw negative attention to ourselves. We need to be ready for the launch."

"Erm... I have some concerns about that sir."

Morton stopped pacing and stared at the speaker on the screen. It was Phil Darcy, the head of the finance department.

"Oh you do, do you Phil? Perhaps you'd like to go through your concerns for us," Morton said in a sarcastic tone.

He stopped pacing beside the big desk in the corner and his hand tightened on an antique brass vase he kept on it. Phil failed to pick up on his boss's tone of voice or the whitening of his knuckles on the vase, but judging by the way the board members on either side of him leant away, everybody else had grasped what was going on here.

"I know I've raised this before," Darcy said. "But are you sure that we're really ready for this? It seems that we are rushing headlong to deliver something that few of us are very clear on the details of." He waved around at his fellow board members. "In fact my people have said that the expenditure on R&D seems to be much higher than budgeted and they can't get any answers when they challenge. They get told that you or Sauer have authorised it and nobody will let them into the details of what it has been spent on."

"Hm. I see. Anything else?" Morton lifted the vase in one hand and held his other to his face in a fist.

"Well, there's..."

Morton cut him off.

"Would you like us all to delay the rest of our day while you moan and whine some more? Shall we delay the launch itself?!" His voice rose in pitch and volume as he spoke until by the end he was almost shrieking. He slammed the vase down on the desk loudly. More than one of the board members flinched even though he wasn't in the room with them. "I've had enough of your constant complaints and negative attitude, Phil. You're fired."

Phil Darcy stared blankly for a moment, unable to take in what had just happened. Eventually he stuttered a response.

"I'm, what? Fired? Just like that? I... you can't do that."

"Yes, Phil. I can. This is my company and I can do as I bloody well please. You can clear your things out now but I want you gone by lunchtime." He turned away from the screen and spoke to the man beside him. "Marcus, contact security and have them meet Darcy in his office and ensure his safe departure."

Marcus Sauer took a couple of steps away from the table, raised a bony hand to his bluetooth earpiece and started muttering quietly to security.

Sauer wasn't even technically a member of the Board, but over the last year or so Morton had come to rely on him more and more. If you asked the other Board members in the safety of their homes most of them would admit to being scared of him. His appearance didn't help and most of them assumed he'd cultivated it on purpose. Originally from Germany, he was very tall which only emphasised how painfully thin he was, and he had a scar on his right cheek that he allowed people to believe he had got in a duel. It moved up and down now while he spoke on the phone and it was hard to take your eyes off it.

In the boardroom downstairs Phil Darcy turned and looked at the others for some support. None came. None of them would even meet his eyes.

"Very well," he said with as much dignity as possible. "It has been a pleasure ladies and gentlemen. Good luck with your launch." He stood and left the boardroom.

Morton waited a moment and then glared at the rest of his team.

"Anybody else have any doubts?" Nobody spoke. "Good, then I suggest we draw this meeting to a close. Get back to work."

The others had started to get up from the table without saying another word by the time Morton switched off the video screen, leaving only him, Sauer and one other person upstairs in his suite.

He put an arm around Sauer's shoulders and walked him to the door.

"I want you to keep a close eye on them, Marcus," he said, dropping into a squat and staring into the tropical fish tank on a table by the door, distracted by the darting movements of the fish.

"Yes sir. Should I start searching for a replacement for Darcy?"

Morton's hand froze where he had been tracing the path of one of the fish. He seemed surprised by Sauer's idea, as though the thought hadn't occurred to him.

"I suppose so, but it isn't your main focus. Darcy leaving does not cause us a problem for the launch. We need some of the others to keep working and you can see doubt on some of their faces. I will not have them causing problems for us. Nothing can be allowed to interfere with the plan."

"Of course sir. Is there anything else?" Sauer asked.

Morton's eyes darted to the corner where the other person was sitting quietly, then he looked back at Marcus and shook his head.

"No."

"Very well, I'll go and see to it." Sauer nodded his skull-like head so low it was almost a bow and left the room.

Morton watched him cross the lobby area through the fancy Venetian glass panels that made up one wall of his apartment. He inclined his head slightly to Morton's private receptionist who worked in the outer room as he passed her and then waited for the lift with his back to her. A moment later, when the doors had closed on Sauer, Morton flicked a switch to darken the glass wall. Then, when he was alone with the person sitting in the corner, his body language changed instantly. His shoulders relaxed and he seemed to shrink slightly.

"Did I do well?" he asked.

"Well enough," came the reply from the corner. "You were right, Darcy isn't necessary for the plan but you must make sure that you are still running the company properly as well. I want it to still be here after the launch."

CHAPTER SEVEN

Jack had asked the Director what was next and the answer turned out to be a trip to one of the rooms they had passed on their way to her office. One with one of the most exciting names. Weapons Development..

"Do I get to have weapons?" Jack asked, so excited he forgot that he was angry at being forced into this. "Spy weapons, like poison dart umbrellas and guns hidden in books?"

Wallace shook his head.

"No guns or poison, no. I can't send a child into the field with weapons like that. But I'm not sending you in defenceless either. I've asked our Weapons Developer to come up with some things that are suitable for someone your age."

They reached the door marked Weapons Development and Wallace held his eye up next to the iris scanner. The door opened and Jack expected to see another office but instead was surprised to see that it opened onto another pure white lift. Wallace stepped inside and went through the same procedure as before, looking up at the camera in the ceiling and stating his name in a flat voice.

"Agent Wallace," the voice seemed to come from all around them although Jack couldn't see any speakers. "Unauthorised guests are not permitted to enter Weapons Development."

The voice sounded reasonable but there would be no arguing with it. The lift refused to move.

Wallace kept looking up at the ceiling and spoke clearly again.

"Plus one is Jack Hawke, temporarily assigned to CIRCLE for one day. Verify with Director."

Wallace looked down at Jack and Jack knew he could speak.

"Just one day?"

"Don't get your hopes up," Wallace said. "It'll take longer than a day but you'll only be on site for one day so the computer only needs to know that. It's state of the art Artificial Intelligence but it can still get confused and if it does we'll be locked in here until Security come for us."

"Oh. That's not good."

"No."

The AI interrupted them.

"The Director confirms Jack Hawke is permitted into Weapons Development until 1500 today. Jack Hawke," Jack was startled at hearing it address him and looked up at the camera like Wallace did. "You must remain accompanied at all times, failure to do so will result in you being secured. Do you understand and accept this?"

Jack decided he liked the snooty tone of the machine even less than he liked it from the Director and almost said 'no' but Wallace nudged him.

"Yes," he said.

"Thank you. You may now proceed to Weapons Development." The lift started moving even as the computer spoke.

The lift moved at the same terrifying speed as the first one but it seemed to Jack as though it went on longer this time. They must be deep underground by now.

"How far down are we going?" he asked.

"I don't know," said Wallace. "This place was originally repurposed decades ago from a proposed underground line that never got finished and it connects to the government nuclear bunker system but I don't know any more than that. Best not to ask too many questions around here, Jack."

That didn't make sense to Jack. In his experience adults seemed fundamentally opposed to asking questions. He didn't like it. And these were spies for God's sake, why wouldn't they want people who asked questions?

After a minute the lift came to a stop and the doors hissed opened and Jack's eyes widened in delight.

It looked like they had reached the lowest level. Through the lift doors he could see that, where the railing had been on the previous floor, there was now a thick glass screen from floor to ceiling. Behind the screen a man was moving inside the pit so this must be the bottom. The man was wheeling a mounted machine gun into view and pointing it at a car. He arranged the belt of ammunition carefully alongside the machine gun and then took up position behind it and aimed it at the car.

Jack held his breath and a smile spread across his face.

And then the view was ruined by a young woman in her mid twenties who stepped into view and blocked their way out of the lift.

"I don't like this Wallace," she said, ignoring Jack as he shifted his position desperately to see past her.

Jack could just about hear a high-speed clicking noise through the soundproof glass so he guessed the man must be firing the gun but he couldn't see a thing. His shoulders fell in disappointment and he gave up and focused on the woman instead.

She had bright purple hair and loads of earrings in her right ear lining it from the lobe to the tip. The bottom one looked like a microchip.

Despite how annoying it was that she had got in the way, Jack had to admit she looked cool.

"I know, Alice, but this is how it needs to be."

"We can't send a child into the field. It's not right." Jack could hear her talking but was transfixed by the piercing he had spotted in her tongue.

"The Director has cleared it. In fact it was her idea."

"Well it's still not right. He could be killed."

They were still in the lift, Alice still blocking their way out with her arms folded.

"He's just doing some reconnaissance," Wallace said.

"He hasn't been trained. Even if he doesn't get himself killed, he'll mess it up."

Jack stepped between them and raised his hands.

"Hey! 'He' is standing right here, thank you. If you've got something to say then say it *to* me, not *about* me."

A small smile twitched the corner of Wallace's face but he got it under control.

"Jack, this is Alice Boothroyd. She is in charge of our Science and Technology division. Everything you see on this level is down to her."

Blimey, thought Jack. *She seems young to be in charge.*

Alice finally looked at him for a split second then just shook her head and walked off. Jack turned back to look at Wallace but before they could speak Alice, still walking away, called back to them.

"Well, are you coming then?"

This time Wallace grinned openly at Jack and gestured for him to follow and the two of them hurried to catch her up.

She continued speaking regardless of the fact that they weren't with her.

"They haven't told me much of what you need to do so I haven't been able to develop any mission specific technology. But I've concentrated on things that might help in general situations and that would not look out of place on a fourteen year old boy."

"Wow! What's that?" Jack interrupted as they passed an open door through which he got a glimpse of a man lifting into the air silently on some sort of air-powered jetpack.

"Not for you," Alice said, stopping in her tracks and reaching back to close the door. "Your stuff is in here."

She led the way into a room three doors down. In the centre of the room was a table with equipment laid out on it. Alice went and stood behind it while Jack and Wallace stood on the other side.

"This is what we've got for you," she said and waved her hand over the table like a magician, which Jack supposed she was really. "The usual assortment of bugs, both video and audio." She pointed to a pile of black tiles no bigger than the nail of his little finger. "The round ones broadcast a signal that's recorded in our secure online area, the square ones record it on themselves. Perfect if you're somewhere without a signal but you do need to be able to collect them again and of course there's a limit to how much they can hold. They'll start recording over themselves after about twenty five hours. Both sorts come with sticky backs, just peel off the paper and stick them somewhere they won't be seen."

"Concentrate on the round ones if you can Jack. We don't want you having to go back anywhere unnecessarily," Wallace said.

Jack nodded.

Alice drew in breath through her nose but whatever she was thinking she kept it to herself.

"Standard issue emergency watch. Press the crown three times in less than a second and it will broadcast an alarm to our people with your location. All our agents have these.

Different designs of course. We got you a digital one, figured that wouldn't be unusual at your age."

"All watches are unusual at my age," Jack said. Nobody he knew wore a watch, everybody used their phone to tell the time.

"Hm. I'll have to think about that," Alice said thoughtfully. "Maybe a change in direction in future. For now, though, you need the watch. Nobody is allowed into the field without one."

"It'll be fine. It's unusual but adults won't realise that and that's what matters."

Alice nodded, quietly impressed with how he was starting to think like an agent.

"Now it starts getting a bit more exciting. The thread in this string bracelet is actually a super-fine high tensile cord. Unwind the bracelet and you have one hundred metres of extremely useful rope. It is incredibly strong under tension, that is to say when something is pulling on it, but it can be cut easily from the side if you need a shorter amount. Agents have used it in the past for abseiling and even on one occasion garrotting someone."

Wallace cleared his throat.

"I'm pretty sure he won't need to garrotte anyone."

"No. No, I should hope not," Alice caught herself. "Moving on. I like this. We are currently developing these," she pointed at a pair of black gloves and posh looking shoes. "Gecko tech. We haven't been able to get them to hold the weight of an adult agent but I think they'll be perfect for you. You weigh what? Seven stone?"

"Seven and a half," Jack replied with a touch of indignation.

"Well, most of our agents are a damn sight bigger than you are. These things are good up to ten stone."

"I can use them to climb walls? Cool!"

"That's the idea. Though you'll still be seen and remember you're not Spiderman. Fall and you'll hit the floor, there's no shooting a web to save yourself. They're currently dress shoes but that won't work for you. Worse than the watch even, right?"

"Yeah, much," Jack thought. Nobody would believe someone his age would wear shoes like that unless they were going to school or a funeral or something.

"Okay, I'll have someone cut them down and attach them to some trainers."

"Can I have a go with them now?"

Alice shot a look at Wallace.

"He'll need to try out a bunch of this stuff to get familiar with it. How long has he got?" she said.

"His permit to be on this level lasts for another couple of hours and then he can practise in the training ground for the rest of today. Mission starts tomorrow."

She shook her head, angry again.

"He needs longer than that. Agents train for weeks with any of our new kit."

"They train for years beforehand too. He's not an agent, Alice, he's just doing a bit of sneaking around. Explain quickly and he'll have more time to practise," Wallace said.

Jack found him interesting. He had seen the doubt in the man's eyes and he was pretty sure that he wasn't really comfortable using Jack like this, but whenever Alice pressed him on it he retreated back into his duty. He'd have to remember that.

"When we're done here I'll have one of my people take you into our test area and demonstrate it all to you, Jack," Alice said, but she was still frosty.

"Thanks," Jack said.

"If it's tomorrow then the shoes might be a problem, but let us know what size you are and we'll see if we can get it done in time. Okay, then, next!" Jack looked down at the table and saw a tracksuit. It was black and there were white stripes down the sides. "Do you know what a wing suit is Jack?"

"For skydiving?"

"That's it. I'm guessing you've never jumped?"

"I've never even been on a plane before let alone jumped out of one." He was worried for the first time, and turned to look at Wallace. "I won't have to go on a plane will I?"

Wallace shook his head. "No," he said.

"There wouldn't be time to train you to jump anyway," Alice said. "But there are plenty of situations where this might be handy and if it isn't then it's just a tracksuit. No harm done."

"Okay."

"If you do need to use it just pull here, and here, like this and..." she demonstrated as she did it and an incredibly thin silk like material shot out of the seams where the white stripes were. There was loads of it.

"Got anything that's more useful on the ground, Alice?" Wallace asked.

Alice shot him a look that would have sent another man running and returned her attention to the table.

"Two more things, Jack. In case you ever need a diversion, or to get away from someone unseen, then you can use these. Smoke grenades." She picked up a set of keys. "There are six of them on the ring. Just drop one of them into water. You can give them a bit of a shake to get the reaction going."

"They're not very big. They can't make much smoke," Jack said. Alice looked at him appraisingly and he felt he needed to clarify. "I mean, the amount of smoke they make has to depend on the volume of the metal, right? That seems logical."

"That's a good point. The earliest versions worked exactly like that and it seriously limited how useful they were, so we changed it up. The smoke isn't really smoke anymore, it's water vapour. So how much smoke they make depends on how much water you put them into."

"Oh. So the keys are just a catalyst. Clever."

Alice looked at Wallace quizzically. She was getting more and more impressed, not to mention surprised, by this boy. Wallace acknowledged her silent point with a wink and a small nod. Jack saw none of it, he was too busy examining the keys.

"Finally then there is this," Alice said to Jack, handing him a mobile phone and interrupting his study.

"I think I've got one of them. Does it make phone calls?"

"Funny, isn't he?" she said lightly to Wallace. Her attitude was slightly warmer now that she saw him as more capable.

"He certainly seems to think so."

"Actually it does make phone calls," she answered Jack. "But it also has a couple of surprises built-in. Put the earphones in and open the compass app and you will find a directional microphone that will let you hear a whisper across a room. If you press the microphone against a wall you will be able to hear what's going on the other side. It works for walls up to about two feet thick depending on what they're made of."

"Neat."

"Yes. Now, turn the camera on as normal and scroll across. After the normal video and slow motion options we've added a night vision function so if you need to see in the dark you'll be able to. Not as good as proper night vision goggles but it'll give you something."

"Don't forget it'll be lit up though so if you're using it then other people can see you," Wallace said.

"I understand."

"Finally, it has a card reader and copier built into it. Our agents report these as particularly useful for impersonating other people. Again you probably won't need it but it's built into the phone anyway. Just open the Space Invader app and hold the phone near a credit card or ID badge and, as long as it has a magnetic strip or a contactless chip, it will take a copy of it. Then you use it by holding it next to the reader you want to fool. Obviously it won't convince a human because it doesn't look like a card but the machine will read it as the card you copied. Anyway, you get the idea... Any questions?"

"I don't think so," Jack said.

"Well, that's it, then. Good luck out there. I'll have one of my people meet you here in a minute or two and take you to the test area to try some of this out."

Later that night, when Wallace had taken Jack back to the foster home, he visited the Director again. There were just the two of them in her office. The Director was pouring herself a drink and waved the crystal decanter at him in a silent offer. He shook his head.

"Was it wise to promise him that you could get his brother released?" he asked.

"Who cares? It's a way of controlling him. I said we had the right lever to pull and we do. Did you see how quickly he went for it?"

"Well, yes, but what happens when you don't do it?"

"By then we'll have what we need. Not getting a conscience are you, Wallace?"

"No, no." Wallace shrugged. He'd been accused of many things in his lengthy career as a spy, most of them true, but never of getting a conscience. Still, this was a kid and it didn't feel quite the same.

"Good. Don't get attached, he's an asset," she said and knocked back her drink in one.

CHAPTER EIGHT

The next day Jack stood outside the ultramodern headquarters of Morton Technology and looked up. It was tall. Very tall. And appeared to be made of a single sheet of glass.

This is what the outside of CIRCLE HQ should look like, well, apart from the Director's office of course. The outside of that should look like the British Museum, he thought.

It was intimidating, he guessed that was the point, but standing here dwarfed by the building he felt very alone. And when he remembered his last conversation with Wallace it didn't help. The well-dressed agent had arranged for someone unconnected to CIRCLE to drop Jack off just in case anyone at Morton Tech recognised their staff, so the last time they had spoken was when the driver picked him up.

"Remember to keep your wits about you," Wallace had said. "You're a smart lad and they'll not be expecting anything funny from you but you're on your own in there. If for some reason we do *absolutely* have to get a message to you we'll pass it along via the SWAT Team IV message board in a book code like Alice's people showed you yesterday. Check the message board at least once every day. That'll seem natural won't it? I mean, you'd be keeping an eye on the board wouldn't you?"

"Definitely. And what about if I absolutely have to get a message to you?" Jack had nodded and asked calmly. He expected an easy answer and was gobsmacked by Wallace's reply.

"You can't I'm afraid. Anything you post will be scrutinised carefully. You can't take the chance. But remember you have the emergency beacon in the watch if you need us to pull you out."

"So I can't get any advice or tell you anything that's happening?"

"No. Radio silence unless you need us to pull you out. Anyway, are you ready?"

Jack had been in shock for most of the journey here and was only now, as he looked up at the tall building, starting to realise what he'd got himself into.

He touched his watch.

Probably a bit early to use it now, he thought. The driver had only just left and he was still standing in the car park. *I can't really claim to have given it my best shot.*

He thought of Bobby, took a deep breath and entered the reception.

The receptionist was on her own so he walked over as confidently as he could manage and stood in front of her.

"Hello, I'm..." he began.

"Jack Dawson," she finished for him using the name that Wallace had selected for him. He'd explained that it was always easier to keep your first name the same so that you reacted properly.

"That's right, how did you?..."

"Oh we do all sorts of magic at Morton Technology," she said with a wink. "And it helps that you're the only appointment I have on my list today who is under twenty!"

"Oh... Oh right." Jack felt stupid but she was being kind about it.

"Dr Sauer will be meeting you and bringing you into the test group."

"Dr Sauer? Not Simon Morton?"

"Oh no my dear, Mr Morton is very busy. He said hello to all of the testers on the first day but because you're joining later Dr Sauer will deal with you. Don't worry though Dr Sauer is Mr Morton's right hand man. Just take a seat there and he'll come and get you soon."

Jack worried for a moment as he sat and waited for Sauer to come and collect him. His plan had been to follow Simon Morton as closely as possible to find out what he could quickly and get back to CIRCLE. He tried his best to stay calm.

It's still okay, he thought. *If Sauer is Morton's right hand man then as long as I stick near him I'll get what I need.*

A minute later an extremely tall man in a hoodie strode across the reception area in his direction.

This must be Sauer. Jack had to try hard not to laugh. The man looked like he'd read somewhere that cool tech executives were wearing hoodies now, but he was so tall and thin that it made him look more like the Grim Reaper than Mark Zuckerberg. The geeky glasses didn't help either.

"Jack Dawson?"

The man smiled and extended his hand to shake Jack's. His grip was surprisingly strong considering his hand felt like a bag of sticks.

"That's right," Jack replied.

"Great! I'm Dr Sauer but you can call me Marcus. Is this all of your stuff?" He gestured to the rucksack that Jack had brought with him.

Jack panicked. Should he have more? Was Sauer going to see through him already?

"Yes, this is mine. Is it, erm, is it okay?"

"Perfect!" the man said with another wide smile. "Come with me then. I'll show you to your room quickly and then we'll get you down to the testing room and introduce you to the others!"

I'm not cut out for this spying stuff, Jack thought. He was already flustered and Sauer had only asked about his luggage.

"Are you excited to be joining us then?" Sauer asked as he escorted Jack up the stairs to his room.

"Definitely. It's a great opportunity." Given how excited Sauer seemed about everything there didn't seem any other response that was appropriate.

"Terrible shame about the girl who had to go home."

"Oh, yeah."

"But her loss is your gain and all that!"

They walked on without speaking for a while. The silence was broken only by the sound of Sauer's shoes on the floor. Jack looked down at them and had to stifle another smile. He was wearing expensive looking black shoes that would have gone better with a tuxedo than the hoodie. In fact Sauer might be the only man who had ever worn a hoodie with shoes so highly polished. They made him think of Alice's final present to him. She had worked her team through the night and when the driver had turned up to collect him he had brought a pair of trainers with him that Jack was wearing now.

Finally the clicking of his heels stopped. Sauer had arrived at Jack's room.

"So, this is where you'll live during the testing," he said and threw open the door dramatically.

Jack stepped into the room and had to hold back a gasp. He had expected it to be fairly basic, but this looked like a well appointed hotel room. A hotel room that someone had crammed with all of the latest technology.

Sauer waited at the doorway while Jack went in and looked around the room.

He ducked into the bathroom, partly to see what it was like but, if he was honest, mostly to get a break from the emaciated doctor. He looked in the bathroom mirror for a minute and sighed. He just didn't know what to make of Sauer. He definitely reckoned that he wasn't a medical doctor or he'd have known he needed a good meal. But that was the least weird thing about him.

He wasn't sure of his plan to stick with him any more either. The way he spoke was exhausting. Everything was an exclamation. Jack had never met one of those religious preachers from American TV but he was pretty sure Sauer would fit right in with them. Apart from the creepy grim-reaper vibe he gave off.

And he had some sort of accent. Jack couldn't quite tell where it came from but combined with his rake thin body, inappropriate hoodie and overly enthusiastic approach it just made him seem even more odd.

He became aware that he'd probably spent too long in the bathroom.

Come on, he's not that weird, he thought to himself. *He's just trying too hard to be friendly. That's not a crime. You're just nervous. You can do this. In fact, maybe I can get something useful straight away.*

He pulled his new phone from his pocket and selected the Space Invader app Alice had shown him the day before. If Sauer was important he'd probably have access to the whole building and that might come in handy. He waited for the app to boot up and then dropped his phone back inside his jacket pocket. Sauer was so tall that it wouldn't be on the same level as the ID badge the man wore around his neck, but it should be close enough to pick it up and get a copy.

He nodded at his reflection and walked out of the bathroom before he could change his mind. He engaged Sauer quickly before he could start talking.

"Can you tell me about the testing itself?" he asked.

"Well, testing is a funny word really! We've done all of the real testing or we wouldn't be where we are now. It's really a PR thing if I'm honest with you, Jack. Do you know what PR is?"

Sauer's cadaverous head swung down to look at him from its perch high on top of his neck.

Do I know what PR is?! Why does no-one seem to grasp that a fourteen year old might know anything? Jack's pep talk to himself in the bathroom had failed miserably. He really didn't like the man. He had hardly ever met anyone more patronising. He had to remind himself that being underestimated was part of the reason he'd been chosen in the first place.

"I think so," he said, putting as much uncertainty into his voice as he could. "Public Relations, isn't it? It's like advertising and stuff to make a company look good. We covered some of it at school."

"That's it, well done! Well, in this case we're using the beta testing as PR by choosing testers who can help spread the word. Some were chosen from schools and businesses in a lottery, like you were. Some are key people we've specially invited. People who are influential in the games industry, YouTubers, media types, that sort of thing."

His ears pricked up at the mention of YouTubers. CIRCLE hadn't told him there'd be YouTubers here. In fact he was beginning to realise that they hadn't really told him much about the testing at all. But then they probably didn't know anything, to them Shark was just a way to get him inside.

"Drop your bag off then and we'll go and meet up with the others! Is there anything in it you want?"

"I..."

"No? Good! Come on then!"

Sauer started heading for the stairs. Luckily for Jack the stairs seemed to take the wind out of Sauer and Jack was able to get a quick question in.

"You mentioned YouTubers?" he said as fast as he could in case Sauer started speaking again.

"Oh yes, some you might know. There's CluelessRebel and Tangy and some others who I confess I've never heard of. YouTube isn't really my thing."

Well, no, Jack thought. *But to be fair I expect they'd only just invented moving pictures when you were my age.*

They reached the bottom of the staircase and Sauer launched back into his rapid fire speech.

"All of your food will be free, you can just help yourself! There are some rules of course. As you'd expect." The head swung back in Jack's direction and waited for some response. Jack nodded and that seemed to be all the trigger Sauer needed. "You can go anywhere on the first floor that you like to visit other testers or whatever but you are not allowed to go anywhere else in the building unaccompanied. You will be collected from your room and escorted to the canteen for breakfast then we'll take you to the gaming room. When you want to go back to your room just ask and one of the staff members will arrange it."

Jack must have looked slightly alarmed because Sauer went on to explain why.

"Morton Tech does a lot of work for the Ministry of Defence, Jack. We can't have state secrets getting into the wrong hands! And that brings me to the next rule! You agreed to strict non-disclosure of anything you learnt here when you entered the competition but we will need you to sign a document today as well. It is very important to us that details of Shark do not leak out until Morton is ready to release them. You can understand that, yes?!"

"Of course," Jack said.

"So... I suppose you want to know about what Shark is don't you?"

"Yes please, they didn't tell us anything at school."

"That's not just your school, Jack. That's everybody! We're keeping it completely secret until the launch day. The only people who know about it are the staff here at Morton Tech who've worked on it and you lucky beta testers. You're really quite privileged to be here!" He paused and Jack nodded but Sauer wasn't looking at him this time. Apparently the pause had been for dramatic effect. "You see these glasses I'm wearing Jack?"

"Erm, yes," he said.

"These are Shark! These and the connection to the Morton Server Cloud. Have you heard of augmented reality? This is augmented reality taken to the next level. Put on a pair of these and you are fully immersed in the Morton world."

"Isn't that more like virtual reality?"

"Great question Jack! No. Virtual reality makes a fake world. Nobody has done it very well yet. Shark takes our world as it is but improves it by adding layers that are indistinguishable from the real thing. Those improvements can be minor tweaks, like showing you directions by laying arrows on top of the road, or they can be a whole new experience like a game. Yes, Jack! A game! That's got you interested hasn't it?" It had, but Sauer was so caught up in his speech he hadn't even looked in Jack's direction. He went on. "That's our first application Jack. Our killer app if you will.

"Do you know that the PC didn't really take off until they developed a spreadsheet? That was their killer app. Technology is cool but nobody would bother buying it if they didn't have a good reason.

"Shark will be able to do all sorts of things in the future but our killer app is the game world we've created. You're going to love it, Jack! Then when launch day comes you can go back to school and we'll give you a free box of Shark glasses to give out to other lucky people in your school. You'll be incredibly popular and we'll find new users!"

He paused and Jack thought some input might be needed from him. He didn't know how conversations with this man were supposed to work. He was beginning to suspect that the odd deaths had just been people who'd spent too much time with Sauer and killed themselves to get a bit of peace. He took a breath to say something but they'd reached a door and Sauer came abruptly to a halt.

"This is it! The gaming room or the GameZone as we call it! Are you ready?"

He threw open the door as he asked, and Jack got his first look at the world's most advanced new gaming platform.

The gaming room turned out to be more like a gaming warehouse. It was massive and had a variety of different parts given over to mock-ups of different real world environments.

There were about thirty people in the room gathered in loose groups. All of them were wearing the Shark glasses. Jack recognised several of the people in the crowd from the YouTube gaming channels he watched.

Sauer strode into the centre of the room and got everybody's attention.

"Guys! Guys! Can I have your attention please? This is Jack Dawson. He's joining us to replace Amrit Patel. Amrit has had to leave as she wasn't well and Jack was the runner up in her school!"

The testers all looked over and some waved, most of them gave him a cursory nod.

"Which team was Amrit on?" Sauer asked one of the supervisors.

"Red team," the woman replied quickly, obviously used to Sauer's style of speech.

"Okay Jack, go and meet your team and remember... enjoy yourself!" Sauer said and turned to leave.

Jack panicked.

"Aren't you staying here?" he said.

"No, no, I have many more responsibilities at Morton Tech than Shark! Sandra and Alex will be able to help you with anything you need from now on."

He walked off and Jack watched him go with a sinking feeling. His first spy plan, to stick close to someone important, had failed completely.

"Okay Jack!" the woman said, clapping her hands and attracting his attention. "I'm Sandra. Let's get you set up. The rest of you do solo play until I've got Jack sorted. Once he's up to speed I'll set up a game."

Sandra led Jack off to a side area with tables full of cutting edge gaming PCs. They made his rig at Frank's look embarrassing.

"You'll need these," she said, handing him a pair of glasses similar to those that Sauer had been wearing. "And sometimes one of these." She gave him a small cylinder with a single button on top.

Jack put the glasses on slowly, expecting everything to change instantly. Nothing happened.

Sandra smiled at him. Everything looked exactly the same.

"What do you think?" She asked.

"Erm... about what? Everything looks the same."

She laughed kindly. "I meant about the fit. Are they comfortable?"

"Oh, erm, yes. They're fine." *I mean, they're glasses, how uncomfortable can they be?* he thought.

"Good. Now watch carefully."

He did and she started shaking her head from side to side so that her long blonde hair swayed backwards and forwards.

"Watching?"

"Yes," Jack said, unable to keep a note of boredom from creeping into his voice.

Then in front of his eyes Sandra flicked her head one way and as she flicked it back her hair changed instantly to a bright green colour.

"Holy crap!" Jack said.

"Notice anything different?"

He tipped the glasses down his nose and looked at her over the top of them. Her hair was exactly the same blonde colour it had been before. He pushed the glasses back up.

"Wow! Move your head," he said, forgetting to be polite. She did so anyway, leaning from side to side and turning in a circle. Her green hair moved with her, perfectly matching the movement of her own. "It's completely seamless."

"Yes."

"And it works in real time?"

"Absolutely. Well, so fast that the human brain can't spot the delay. Keep watching." She grinned and stuck her tongue out at him. As soon as she did her features morphed into those of a devil. She laughed and the devil face moved in perfect time with hers. "What do you think?"

"Oh my God, it's amazing. What about sound?"

"Bone inductor speakers in the legs of the glasses," the devil said. "Almost impossible to tell apart from the real world. You wouldn't know it wasn't real. Tell me something you'd like to hear. Birdsong? Sirens? Door shutting?" she was scrolling down a list on her tablet. She hadn't turned the devil face off and it looked completely weird.

"A siren."

She tapped something on her tablet and Jack heard a faint siren off to his right. It was so realistic that he couldn't help himself, he turned his head slightly towards it. The devil was grinning now. The siren seemed to approach and pass right in front of him then disappear off to his left. It was uncanny.

"It's amazing. There's no other word. The gaming world is going to go mad for this." Jack meant it. He'd like to be a good enough spy to fake the excitement he was feeling but he didn't need to be. Shark truly was state of the art.

"It is, isn't it?" Sandra said.

"What about this?" He waved the little cylinder she had handed him.

"Depends on the game. It isn't needed for most of the AR things but for lots of games you need a weapon or a tool. Shark will sense where that remote is and it'll turn into whatever the game demands."

Jack shook his head.

"This is so cool," he said and then caught himself. *I've got to stay focused,* he thought. *I'm not really here for this.*

Sandra smiled, clearly used to this sort of reaction.

"Okay, let's get you into your team and have some fun."

Well, a quick game won't hurt. I need to blend in after all.

CHAPTER NINE

Sandra took him to one side of the warehouse and introduced him properly to his team. They all smiled and said hello, two of them even came and stood by him and clapped him on the back.

"Everybody gather round please," Sandra called out and gradually they stopped what they were doing and shuffled over. It was noticeably less quick than when Marcus had done it earlier. Obviously Marcus made everybody else here as uncomfortable as he made Jack. Eventually they were all together. "Great. So this morning we're going hunting. Glasses on folks."

Jack looked around. She almost hadn't needed to say anything at all. There were only half a dozen people who ever took them off. Jack's own glasses were still on from earlier. She waited until everybody had them on and then began. The glasses made her tablet appear to be a wand and she waved it with a dramatic flourish. Jack knew that it was really still a tablet and he guessed that when it looked like she was waving it then in the real world she was tapping on it but it was masked completely.

When she'd finished spinning the wand she was dressed in a medieval princess costume. She looked at herself and laughed loudly.

Jack looked down at himself through his glasses and saw that he was dressed like a hunter. He was wearing a leather tunic and his remote had become a crossbow. Everybody around him had changed into what looked like a character from Lord of the Rings. Including some who had turned into orcs or elves or other mythical creatures he didn't recognise.

Sandra carried on explaining the game to them.

"You'll be hunting scrawns. They look like this," she said and waved her wand over her outstretched left hand. A cute little ball of fur appeared hovering above her hand and spun on the spot so they could all get a good look at it. "Cute aren't they? But be warned they're tricky little creatures and they pack a mean bite. If one of them gets to touch you, then you're out of the game." The imaginary scrawn opened its mouth wide and displayed a razor sharp set of tiny teeth.

"There'll be twenty or so scrawns, the computer will pick the exact number. When they've all been found I will sound a note on this horn and the game will end. You'll operate in your usual teams. You get 20XP for killing a scrawn yourself and everybody on the team who gets the most scrawns will earn 500XP each. Form up!"

Everybody moved around until there were two big groups facing each other. Because he'd been talking to Sandra, Jack ended up near the front of his team, looking across the gap in the centre to the other team. In the front of the Blue Team he spotted a YouTuber he followed and couldn't stop himself from saying hello.

"Hey, you're RedRob aren't you?" he asked.

"Yeah. Although Red Robin Hood might be a better name right now," the man replied with a kind smile, gesturing down at himself. He was dressed like Jack but had a longbow instead of Jack's crossbow.

"Wow. I follow your channel, man. This is an honour. My name's Jack."

"Yes, yes. An honour," said the boy standing next to RedRob, irritation dripping off him. He was about seventeen and had a heavy French accent. When he said 'honour' it sounded more like 'onnurrr', but Jack understood. "Can we get on with the game now?"

"Sure. Sorry. I was just saying hello," Jack said.

The French boy looked at him, obviously annoyed that Jack had answered back at all.

"Well, say hello to your own team Jackie, we are the opponents."

"Sorry? What was that? I couldn't make it out through your bad accent," he said, innocently. Jack genuinely hadn't understood the last word but he spoke French well enough that if he had really wanted to understand what the guy was saying he could have spoken to him in his own language. But since he was obviously being an arse he didn't bother.

"We are opponents!" the boy repeated.

Jack gave the boy a big smile.

"Ohhhh, opponents. Anyway," he said and purposefully angled himself to face RedRob with his eyes wide. Then he casually flicked his head towards the French boy. "I guess sportsmanship is not big in Spain then! Good luck."

RedRob didn't have time to answer because the boy pushed forward to stand in front of Jack.

"Spain?! I am French, you little cochon!"

Jack understood but didn't respond to the insult. He just shrugged as though he had no idea what the other lad was talking about.

Sandra chose that moment to intervene before it got any further out of hand.

"Okay chaps, that'll do," she said. "We're all here to have fun. Is everybody ready to start?"

There was a chorus of yeses (and one 'Oui' from Sebastien who was now determined to emphasise his French-ness).

A girl on Jack's team muttered quietly from behind him so that only Jack could hear.

"You shouldn't have done that. He's a top class idiot but he carries a lot of weight here."

Jack turned, she was about his age, maybe a year older than him and through his glasses she appeared to be an angelic looking blonde she-elf. He raised his glasses so he could see what she really looked like. She looked almost the same but without the pointed ears and the leather tunic and velvet cloak she wore in the game was just a pair of ripped jeans and a t-shirt.

"What's his problem? Who does he think he is?" Jack asked.

The elf-girl laughed with a sound like bells playing.

"His name is Sebastien Lefevre and that's exactly his problem. No-one here knows who he is but everyone gets excited about the YouTubers. His mother is the French president and his grandad was Mayor of Paris or something so he thinks he's like French political royalty."

"Oh. Does he remember what they did to their royalty?"

The girl laughed again.

"Maybe don't remind him."

Jack turned back to face Sandra just in time for her to shout "Go!" and wave her wand dramatically.

The GameZone instantly transformed into an enchanted forest. Trees and bushes took the place of the obstacles that Jack remembered were there in real life.

Absolutely amazing! he thought.

Most of the testers scattered instantly but some of them chose to stay in the grassy clearing that the centre area had now become. Jack turned back to the elf-girl and saw that she was one of the ones who'd stayed. She was in a crouch with a longbow drawn and was tracing the arrow around, looking for a target.

"Team up with me?" he said.

"We're already on the same team, genius," she replied with a smirk.

"Yeah but I mean you've played this before and I haven't, can I stick with you and learn the ropes?"

The girl appeared to consider it for a moment then decided better of it.

"Tell you what. Prove you're worth it first and you can hang round with me next time."

Then she pulled her cloak around herself and was gone.

She literally vanished in front of Jack's eyes.

He peered over the top of his Shark glasses and saw her running off but in the game the glasses made her cloak of invisibility work perfectly. In real life she disappeared around one of the corners and he lost her.

Charming, Jack thought.

He looked around to see if there was anybody else he could tag along with but, while he was trying to find someone who looked approachable, one of the little scrawns ran right in front of him.

He chased off after it, racing against a girl from the Blue Team. She was dressed as a wizard but he didn't recognise her. The pair of them fired shot after shot at the scrawn as they ran, the stars from the girl's wand whizzing alongside Jack's crossbow bolts.

The race lasted about thirty seconds before Jack caught the scrawn with a lucky shot and it disappeared in an explosion of sparks. Almost simultaneously a loud voice echoed through the artificial trees.

"First kill of the game by Jack Dawson for Red Team. Well done Jack. Welcome to Morton Tech!"

Around him he heard a mix of cheers and groaning rise up. It wasn't hard to guess which side were doing which.

"Well done Jack, good shot," said the Blue Team wizard he had beaten to the kill. Jack didn't have time to reply before the girl had run off in search of other prey.

With the first kill under his belt, Jack found himself drawn more completely into the game. It was so good that Jack almost forgot why he was at Morton Tech at all, but halfway through it dawned on him that he wasn't really supposed to be focusing on Shark. He didn't think that there was much point in bugging the GameZone but he knew he should practise so, as he moved around the game, he planted four of the bugs.

It was as easy as Alice's staff had shown him in the CIRCLE test area and by the time he put the fourth one into place he was quite pleased with himself. He had got it down to one slick move that, unless someone was watching very carefully, should look quite natural.

Finally he reached another clearing at the top of a huge waterfall. He smiled at how clever the game was when he saw the waterfall. He'd wondered how they'd avoid people running into walls while they were playing the game and this must be their answer. They must have some sort of barrier that fitted into the game and marked the edge of the game world.

He edged slowly as close as he dared to it and peered over the top. It disappeared beneath him into a cloud of mist.

Clever, it really does make you feel uncomfortable, he thought as he came away from the edge quickly and sat down on a fallen tree.

Although he hadn't seen a scrawn for ages himself, at the top right corner of his glasses there was a little counter that told him there were still four left, so he had just decided to attach one last bug under the tree and go hunting again when he heard a clanking noise.

He looked in the direction of the noise and a knight in full body armour stepped from the trees.

"Hail fair knight!" Jack said with a smile in what he hoped was game appropriate language.

The knight didn't reply. Instead it kept walking straight up to him and, without stopping, pushed him. Hard.

Jack tumbled backwards off the tree and landed with thump on the ground. It didn't particularly hurt but he couldn't believe anyone would do it.

"Hey! What do you think you're doing?!" he said.

"You need to learn manners, English," the knight said as he raised his visor to show his face. It was the French boy, Sebastien.

Sebastien stepped over the tree and loomed above Jack, standing so close that Jack could not get up.

Jack was angry. If this had been any other situation then he would have had a proper fight with Sebastien and done as much damage as quickly as he could. Jack wasn't big but he had studied Brazilian Jiu-Jitsu for years and he was a green belt, the highest you could get before you were sixteen. Bobby had taught him to stick up for himself, and any time someone had tried to bully him before he'd done exactly that and stopped it before it began. But this was different. He had a job to do. How would CIRCLE react if he got kicked out of Morton Tech before he could find anything out for them? They wouldn't help Bobby, that was for sure. Besides, Jack *Dawson* probably didn't know Brazilian Jiu-Jitsu.

He shuffled backwards with a clumsy crab-like movement to try to get room to stand up but Sebastien kept pace with him.

I need to calm this down, Jack thought.

"I didn't know who you were," he said.

Then with a sinking feeling, he realised that would probably only make things worse. It did. Sebastien's nostrils flared like an angry horse and he breathed in with a hiss as he started walking forward again. Jack was forced to scramble back further or get parts of him stood on that he'd really rather not.

"The people in this country know *nothing!*" Sebastien said. "Nothing of any importance at all. You are all so obsessed with your social media and your McDonald's culture you stole from America."

Jack kept moving backwards and became aware of the growing noise coming from the waterfall. He estimated he must be about four feet from the edge.

Sebastien face twisted into an ugly sneer.

"You know what happens if you die in Shark, right English? It is so realistic that your mind convinces your body. You will have a heart attack and die."

Jack couldn't believe his ears. Surely Sebastien wasn't really going to kill him just because he didn't know who he was?! But then he thought of the few spoilt little rich kids he'd known and it fitted uncomfortably into a pattern. The sense of entitlement and privilege and, even more than that, the certainty that whatever nasty crap you might pull, mummy and daddy would protect you. He still didn't think it was likely but it *was* just about possible.

By now they had reached the edge of the cliff and Sebastien was still standing above him giving him nowhere to go.

Jack glanced over his shoulder and could see the water churning far below where the waterfall crashed down onto the rocks. If he fell down something like that in real life then it would definitely kill him and if his mind believed that then...

He did not want to die. He had to act now.

He stopped moving backwards and pulled his legs underneath him, getting into an awkward crouch ready to spring at Sebastien.

"Oh no you don't," Sebastien said with a murderous look in his eyes. "You're going for a swim. Bye-bye Jackie!"

He raised his foot, planted it squarely on Jack's chest and pushed before Jack had time to jump.

Jack could do nothing, he stumbled backwards over the cliffside and screamed.

Less than a second later his back hit the floor of the warehouse and all of the air rushed from his lungs.

Jack lay there winded, totally unable to work out what was going on.

His stomach felt like it did when he woke up after one of those falling dreams.

Sebastien was still standing above him but now he was pointing down at Jack and laughing loudly.

All at once the Shark world disappeared. The enchanted forest melted and the GameZone snapped back into view.

An announcement came over the speakers.

"The Hunting of the Scrawn is over. Jack Dawson and Sebastien Lefevre, please remain where you are."

Jack struggled up, ignoring the sick feeling in his stomach and looked around. Everybody was coming out of the game with a blink and as soon as they did they turned to stare at him.

Sebastien was still laughing at him and pretty soon others joined in.

Just briefly, he wished he had died for real.

After the embarrassment died down Sandra explained to Jack that Sebastien had been lying to him. Shark couldn't kill you. The worst that would happen when the game world and the real world were out of sync was that you'd get a bad case of seasickness.

Jack felt like an idiot but at least he hadn't been in real danger. He also decided if he could find a way to get back at Sebastien without endangering his mission then he would.

More importantly he decided that there was no way he was going to get anything useful for CIRCLE by staying in the GameZone. He'd probably wasted the bugs he'd planted but he didn't feel too bad about that as they'd given him plenty. He felt in his pocket. It felt like he still had about ten or so in there, and he knew there were thirty more hidden in a secret compartment in the bottom of his bag upstairs.

They'd said all they wanted him to do was try his best but he didn't really believe them. If he did this but didn't find anything useful he didn't trust the Director to honour her word. He knew how people in power worked. They wouldn't help Bobby if he didn't help them.

Despite what Sauer had said about it being forbidden, he was going to have to explore the rest of the building. And he was going to have to do it as soon as he could.

When she'd finished taking care of him, Sandra and the other assistant, Alex, decided it was time to have lunch to give the testers time to settle down after Jack's outburst.

They all filed to the canteen like infant children on a school trip, grabbed whatever food they wanted and took a seat. Most people hung around with their teams so Jack did the same. The elf-girl from earlier ended up sitting next to him.

"Told you you shouldn't have wound him up," she said.

"You were right."

She nodded as though she hadn't expected anything else.

"He's just a spoilt brat," a guy in his late twenties or early thirties said and turned around.

Jack recognised him. He was Veteran, a famous player and streamer of SWAT Team IV. Jack subscribed to his feed. He couldn't believe he hadn't spotted him earlier.

"Yeah, a brat. Aren't you Veteran?" he said trying to keep it cool.

"I am. Do you play?"

He meant SWAT Team IV.

"A bit. Nothing like you though."

"Maybe we'll have to have a quick game while we're here if we can get Sandra to set us up with a connection."

"That would be great." Jack tried not to sound totally desperate.

"Cool, I'll have a chat with her later and see if we can sort something."

"Thanks," Jack grinned.

Oh well, if I fail completely then at least I've got to play with Veteran, he thought.

It was the first thing that had really cheered him up since he'd got here.

CHAPTER TEN

There was another organised game after lunch in which Jack did his best to keep away from Sebastien, but the French boy seemed to have lost interest in him anyway. After that they played solo games. When the games weren't organised the place was a lot more relaxed and the staff hardly watched them at all. Jack decided that it was his best chance to explore the rest of the site.

He took off his glasses and waited for anyone to notice. They didn't. He glanced over at the staff and saw that they were all playing as well. Depending on how immersive their games were they might not be able to see him at all.

He tested it by getting up and walking around the warehouse.

If anyone asks I'll just say I'm stretching my legs.

Nobody asked. Everybody was lost in their Shark glasses so nobody paid him any attention.

He gradually made his way over to the doors and stood there for a minute. He could feel his heart pounding in his chest. Right now he was just a tester who had got a bit bored and needed to take a walk. When he stepped through this door it would be a lot more difficult to explain.

He took one last look at the staff area. None of them were looking in his direction.

He opened the door just enough to fit through and slipped through the gap. Then he closed it as quietly as he could and stood in the corridor for a moment breathing heavily.

Now what am I supposed to do? he thought. He put his hand in his pocket and felt the incriminating presence of the bugs. He'd have to plant them but where? CIRCLE hadn't given him any idea of where they really wanted the things.

He thought about where the three people who had died had come from. Maybe he'd start with their departments.

The one thing in his favour was that thousands of people worked here so if anyone didn't recognise him it wouldn't raise the alarm straight away. It also meant that there were signs everywhere.

He saw one that pointed to Systems Architecture. He had no real idea of what it meant, but the woman who'd ridden her horse off a cliff had worked there, so he headed in that direction.

It was like being back in CIRCLE HQ with room after room with weird-sounding names.

This place is massive, he thought a minute later as he was still trudging up the corridor.

Just then a group of workers came out of a door ahead of him and started to walk in his direction. They all looked old and he suddenly realised that he must stand out like a sore thumb. This wasn't a school. Apart from the GameZone this was a place of work. Everybody would be an adult.

He started to bend his head to look at the floor repeating, *Don't look at me, don't look at me,* in his head like a mantra. Then he remembered Wallace's incredibly short instructions on spy-craft.

"Always try to look confident wherever you are. Most people will just assume you should be there," he'd said.

Jack raised his head and made a massive effort to keep looking at the little group, he picked the man closest to him and looked him directly in the eye.

"Afternoon," he said as he passed them. He had made his voice as deep as possible but to his own ears it sounded like a strangled gasp. He must have pulled it off though because they simply nodded politely and kept walking in the other direction.

It works! he thought.

After that he held himself up straight and walked as confidently as he could, but he didn't see anybody else before he got to Systems Architecture.

He placed his hand on the handle to open the door and then froze.

What if there's someone in there?

He looked around nervously, hoping nobody would come into the corridor and held his ear to the door. He couldn't hear anything but he had no way of knowing how thick the door was. Morton Tech were a defence contractor after all, for all he knew they could make all of their doors soundproof.

Then he remembered his phone.

He pulled it from his pocket, stuck the earphones in and opened the compass app. Then he checked no-one was nearby again and pressed the edge against the door.

At first there were odd scratching noises but then he realised that he was moving the phone slightly. He held it as still as he could and held his breath.

Nothing.

Should he trust it or was he about to walk into a room full of Systems Architects (whatever they were)?

He risked it and opened the door a crack. He still couldn't hear anything so he opened it further and peeped through the door. It was empty so he dived inside before anyone could see him in the corridor.

The room gave him no clue what a Systems Architect would do. There were a bunch of desks with computers on and a giant whiteboard at the front covered in diagrams and lists of things he didn't understand. It had probably been a bit much to hope that one of them would be titled "Evil Plan". None of them were.

He fished a bug from his pocket and stuck it underneath one of the computer desks closest to him and hurried back to the door. He opened it just enough to peep out and check that nobody was there. The corridor was still empty. He opened the door fully and was about to run out when he spotted the name plate on the room opposite. It said 'Boardroom'.

That's where the people who run the company all meet up, he thought. *That has to be useful.*

He got his phone out ready and flicked to the listening app, checked one last time that nobody was coming and dashed over to the boardroom. He went through the same process with his phone, holding it against the door and listening carefully through the earbuds. It sounded empty so he threw open the door and shot inside as fast as he could.

He let out a big breath and leant his back on the door.

This is too scary.

Once he had caught his breath he took a good look around the room. There was a massive table in the centre, a bar on the side with fruit and biscuits and a fridge, and then a huge video screen on one wall. The chairs around the board table were dark leather and could have eaten you whole.

How the other half live, Jack thought.

There was no "Evil Plan" meeting agenda here either but at least he was sure having a bug inside this room would give CIRCLE something useful. He moved as quickly as he could, dropping to his knees and crawling under the table.

When he was under the middle he peeled off the sticker and stuck one of the audio bugs in place.

He climbed back out and took another look around, where would be best to put one of the video bugs? On top of the video screen. They'd probably all be looking that way, wouldn't they? He glanced at his watch, he'd only been away from the GameZone for seven minutes so far. He couldn't believe it, it felt like forever. Even so, he'd better not be much longer. He hurried over to the screen but found he couldn't reach the top.

They should get taller agents, he thought.

He stuck the bug on the bottom of the screen. There was no way to check so he'd just have to hope it would have a good enough angle to get the whole table.

He hurried back to the door, stepped back into the corridor and started heading back to the GameZone.

He had only got three steps away from the boardroom door when a voice called out his name.

"Mr Dawson, is it?!"

Jack froze on the spot and his heart sank. Being seen wasn't good. Being seen by someone who knew his name was worse. Being seen by someone who knew his name and spoke with that weird, excited accent was just about the worst.

He turned and saw the three men coming towards him. Jack had never seen two of the men before but, as he'd feared, the one in the middle was Sauer. He was wearing a black suit now. It looked much better on him than the hoodie, and at least his shoes matched it, but he still managed to look like an emissary of death. Jack imagined he'd had the cloth for the suit cut from the night sky by a demon or something.

"Oh hello," he said, trying to sound relaxed, even though he imagined Sauer could see his heart beating just by looking at his neck.

"You should not be out here without supervision from the staff."

"Oh I'm sorry. I came out to find the toilet."

"The toilet?" Sauer repeated. He looked unconvinced.

"Yes, everybody was playing a solo game and I needed to go. I couldn't find any inside the GameZone." It sounded weak even to him. Then a flash of inspiration hit him. "I was in a forest simulation and it wasn't until I came out here that I realised the Shark glasses were probably hiding the toilets from me."

Sauer still looked annoyed but his features softened a little as though he found it a bit more believable now.

"Ah, well. Perhaps you will have to add that to your feedback. Must have toilets clearly marked in all game worlds!"

He finished with a flash of his artificial enthusiasm from earlier and Jack tried to join in.

"Ha, yes!" he said.

Judging by the way the man narrowed his sunken eyes, Jack's attempt had been too clumsy.

Sauer started walking down the corridor again, his men fell in beside him and Jack was swept along with them. At first no-one spoke and the only sound was the echoing of Sauer's shoes hitting the floor. After a moment though Sauer began to speak, though this time his tone had none of the excitement Jack had found so exhausting earlier.

"Do you remember the rules Jack? If you come out here without a member of staff then you won't be able to get back in. It wouldn't be wise to get found wandering the corridors at Morton Tech. We work with the Ministry of

Defence and some of the things on site here are strictly top secret. We have rules for a reason Jack."

"Yes, of course, sorry," Jack said and meant it, although what he was really sorry for was getting caught.

By now they had walked back to the GameZone entrance and were standing outside the door.

"From now on you'll stay inside the game area at all times unless a member of staff lets you out. Understood?"

"Completely."

Sauer stared at Jack and didn't speak. He was in the way of the door. Jack found himself wishing for Sauer's over-the-top cheerfulness to come back. Emotionless Sauer was unsettling.

"So... can you open it for me?" Jack asked.

"Yes of course." Sauer opened the door and held it for Jack. Jack started to walk through and Sauer caught his shoulder as he walked past. "Did you forget you came out for the toilet, Mr Dawson?"

"Oh. Erm. Yes."

One eyebrow slid up the paper thin skin covering Sauer's skull. "Do you not need it any more?"

"I'll go when I'm back inside," Jack stammered out.

Sauer let go of his shoulder and stood aside for Jack to pass.

"Okay, well remember to take your glasses off so you can find it!" His voice was loud enough for others in the GameZone to hear and was back to super friendly.

"Thanks," said Jack as he practically fell through the door with relief.

"Enjoy the rest of the day Mr Dawson!"

Sauer turned back to his colleagues and the door swung closed automatically behind him.

Jack let out a deep breath and waited for his heart to slow to a rate that might not kill him. Gradually he became aware of the space outside of his chest. The solo game was still going on but some of the testers had finished their games and were sitting around. The elf-girl was one of them. She walked up to him, took his arm casually like they already knew each other and led him to an area where they couldn't be overheard. Then she spoke as though she were continuing their earlier conversation.

"It wouldn't be a good idea to upset *him* either," she said.

"I wasn't trying to," Jack said.

"Hm. Got a knack for getting in trouble haven't you?"

"So it would seem." Jack stuck his hand out. "I'm Jack. I like video games and, apparently, getting in trouble."

"I'm Abi, I like puzzles and stupid people really get on my nerves. Don't turn out to be a stupid person or I'll be very disappointed," she replied with a smile and shook his hand. "So why were you outside?"

"I needed the toilet."

"And you couldn't use the toilets in here?" she asked, looking puzzled.

"That's what Sauer said."

"Well, he's got a point."

She clearly didn't believe him and Jack decided to take a chance. He couldn't stand the idea of doing this on his own. His run-in with Sauer had proved that. He needed an ally and Abi had been nice to him so far. Besides she had been here longer than he had, she might well have seen something that could help him narrow down his search.

His eyes darted around the GameZone to check no-one was listening to them and lowered his voice.

"You might think I'm crazy but I think there's something going on here."

Abi looked around as well, unconsciously copying him to make sure they weren't being overheard. When she answered him it was in a whisper.

"What do you mean?" she asked.

"It's odd isn't it, a defence contractor suddenly deciding to make computer games?"

She tilted her head thoughtfully.

"I suppose it is."

Jack was relieved that she wasn't treating him like he was insane.

"Have you seen anything odd before I got here?"

"Like what?"

"I don't know exactly. Anyone acting suspiciously."

"Not that I can think of, we're mostly kept in here."

"I'm going to find out what's going on."

"Why?"

Jack hesitated. That had thrown him. She asked it so simply that he didn't know how to answer. There was no way he could tell her about CIRCLE. The truth seemed ridiculous: *A secret government agency has recruited me and I want to save my older brother from going to jail for a crime I planned.* No, this wasn't one of those times where honesty was the best policy. He made something up on the spot.

"I want to be a reporter when I'm older and this would make a great story."

"If there really is something going on here, you mean."

"Yes, but that's why I need to find out."

"Okay. How?"

Again Jack hesitated but he felt like he could trust this girl. Twice now she had come to check he was alright when she didn't have to.

"I've got some bugs that I'm going to plant around the place and see if I can learn anything from them."

"You've got bugs?!" Abi sounded excited, and not in the creepy Sauer-way. "Where did you get them from?"

Jack thought quickly, "An online gadget shop in Omaha in the US. You can get anything off the internet."

Abi accepted that.

"Wow. Is that what you were doing out there when Sauer brought you back?"

"Yeah."

"Double wow. That is so cool. Where did you plant them?"

Jack shrugged, having someone to talk to would help keep him sane in here but he didn't think a spy would share a list of the places he'd bugged.

"Just around," he said. "I don't know exactly what I'm looking for so I'm covering everywhere I can."

Abi looked at him thoughtfully.

"You're going back out aren't you?"

That had been his plan but how did she know?

"No," he said.

"I can help. Take me too."

"I said I'm not doing it again."

She ignored him. "It'd be better to do it at night. I'll meet you under the main staircase in reception at fifteen minutes past midnight."

CHAPTER ELEVEN

Jack got back to his room that evening and fell through the door with a big breath. It was becoming a pattern.

I can't believe how close that was, he thought. *Sauer is definitely suspicious of me now. I'll have to watch that.*

He kicked off his shoes and threw himself onto his bed. He lay there and stared at the ceiling, thoughts tumbling through his head.

Should I have told Abi? He just didn't know. She hadn't taken no for an answer and in the end he'd agreed to take her along that night. He couldn't help but feel pleased to have someone else involved but he couldn't tell her anything about CIRCLE so maybe he should have just kept it to himself. What if she asked a question he didn't know how to answer?

I could always just tell her I'm giving up, he thought. Another advantage of being a kid was that people expected you to get fascinated with things and then drop them. He could just throw himself into the Shark game world and tell her he wasn't interested in finding anything odd any more.

Suddenly somebody knocked on the door and he sat bolt upright.

Who could that be?

Whoever it was knocked again but it didn't sound angry. More polite than anything.

He jumped up off his bed and opened the door carefully.

"Hello," he said.

"Good afternoon." A young woman wearing a Morton Tech ID badge stood there with a big smile on her face. "You've got an invitation from Mr Morton for dinner this evening."

She held out a cream envelope as she spoke but Jack didn't take it. He just froze, his face slowly going white as the blood drained from it.

Why does Morton want to see me?

"Why?" he asked.

He had tried to sound as natural as he could but the girl looked surprised. Obviously nobody ever asked that question.

Damn it, thought Jack, *I need to get better at hiding my reactions.*

"I don't know," she said. "I'm just delivering your invitation." She stood with her hand still outstretched, the invitation still clasped firmly in it where Jack had not taken it.

"Right. Yes, of course. Sorry." Jack finally took the invitation from her hand. "Thank you for this."

"That's okay," she said. "I hope you have a good evening."

She turned to leave but Jack called her back.

"Oh, wait! I'm sorry. What should I wear?"

"I don't know, but if there's a dress code then maybe the invitation will tell you?"

Then she left, confused by the strange boy who wouldn't want dinner with one of the most famous men in the country.

Jack propped the invitation up on his dressing table and stared at it. He'd have to open it in a minute, even if just to find out if he was supposed to dress up smartly but he couldn't bring himself to yet.

Why was Morton inviting him to dinner?

Sauer must have seen me come out of the boardroom and gone back and found the bugs.

Should he push the alarm button on his watch? If they'd found out what he was doing then he was in serious trouble.

But then surely they wouldn't have invited me to dinner.

Eventually he opened the envelope and found a posh card invitation. It told him to dress casually (*Whatever that means,* he thought) but it didn't give him any clue as to whether they'd found him out.

He lay back onto his bed and closed his eyes again but there was no way he was falling asleep.

The lift doors opened on to Morton's penthouse suite and Jack stepped out. A receptionist was sitting opposite the lift doors.

His own company and his own receptionist, Jack thought. *I don't care if he is doing something evil, I want this when I'm older.*

She glanced at her screen and presumably the computer told her who he was because she greeted him by name.

"Good evening Mr Dawson."

He'd never been called Mr Dawson so much in his life.

Ha! he thought, *I've never been called that because it isn't my name!* But nobody had called him Mr Hawke either.

"Erm, evening," he said. "I'm here for... erm... I've got this..."

He pulled his invitation hesitantly from his pocket.

"Mr Morton's meal." The receptionist said smoothly. "You're the last to arrive, go on in."

The last, thought Jack. *That must mean I'm not alone. That's got to be good, right?*

He headed in the direction that the receptionist had waved, trying to remember Wallace's advice to hold his head up and look confident. It wasn't easy. The penthouse was designed to show off wealth and power. As he opened the door the first thing he saw was a big old fashioned partner desk made of dark wood, placed in front of a window. The desk would have been impressive if he hadn't just been sitting in front of the CIRCLE Director's desk. That made this one look a bit puny in comparison, but Morton's view through the window more than made up for it. You could see for miles.

A noise from the other side of the colossal room drew his attention and he turned to see a long table like the one in the boardroom. This one was set for dinner and with a huge sense of relief he saw how many people were already sitting around it. There was Sandra and Alex, and Sauer too, Jack noticed with a groan, but happily what looked like the whole of the red team were there as well.

Oh, thank God! he thought. *If he's invited all of them it can't be anything to do with me.*

There were several loud conversations going on around the table and none of the team looked up.

There were two spare seats, one was beside Morton and one was in front of him. Jack supposed that was a good thing. If they didn't suspect him after all then the closer he was to Morton the better.

At that Morton looked up.

"Ah, you must be Jack Dawson?" he said, Jack nodded. "Come and sit beside me."

Jack walked around the table and Morton pulled the chair out for him, smiled and then picked up a spoon and hit it gently against his glass so that it rang out like a crystal bell.

"Friends!" he shouted and the other conversations came to an abrupt halt and everybody looked in his direction. Sitting next to him Jack was uncomfortable to have all of those eyes staring at him even though he knew they were really looking at Morton. "Thank you all for coming this evening."

Jack tuned out Morton's words and looked along the table to see where Abi was sitting. He realised with a sinking feeling that she wasn't there.

Oh no, has she done something stupid because of what I said? Did they catch her?

Jack was in turmoil. He didn't know whether to ask someone about Abi or not. An argument was running in his head and he couldn't stop it.

It might seem innocent if he was interested in a new friend but if they really had caught her then he could ruin his cover by being connected to her.

But if they'd got her then it was his fault. He had to do something.

Then he imagined the Director's face and thought of Bobby.

He had to stick to this whatever the cost.

He decided to keep quiet and check on her after the meal. Maybe there was an innocent explanation.

Maybe.

He'd been lost in his worries about Abi but now he became aware that Morton was wrapping up his speech.

"Anyway, it is not long now until our launch and you will all get free samples of Shark to take back to be heroes to your organisations! Well, that's enough talk from me, your food is getting cold! Eat up and enjoy it but if you'll take some advice from me you'll leave room for dessert. Our on-site chef is a bit of a pudding specialist."

When everybody had started eating again and conversation had risen to a background hum that made it impossible to hear anyone but your immediate neighbours, Morton leant towards Jack and spoke in a low voice.

"I heard something about you today that worried me Jack."

Jack froze with his fork halfway to his mouth and his eyes went wide.

Oh God, he knows! Sauer found the bugs or caught Abi doing something and they know all about me.

"What was that?" he said keeping his voice as light as he could.

"The staff told me that our young French VIP, Sebastien, was unkind to you. I'm afraid I can't say I'm surprised. I've had a little to do with his mother when I've been lobbying for Morton Tech in France and she is an unpleasant woman as well. She'll be here for the launch so you can judge for yourself."

Relief washed over Jack. He knew how to handle this. He didn't believe in dobbing people in. He could handle his own problems. And this conversation might give him the perfect opportunity to get a bug as close to Morton as anyone ever could.

He slipped his hand innocently into his pocket, picked out one of the bugs and held it in his palm with his thumb.

"He's alright, he's just making a point. I'm the new boy. I've dealt with people like him before," he said turning to face Morton as naturally as he could.

"Oh really, when?"

Jack hesitated, he'd had plenty of run-ins with bullies himself but would Jack *Dawson* have dealt with bullies? Did you get bullies at the sort of schools he was supposed to go to? He remembered what Wallace had told him to make sure that if he had to lie he should keep it as close to the truth as possible so he didn't get caught out.

"Well," he said. "Not exactly like him, none of them were the sons of presidents, I can't say I've ever met one of them before." As he spoke he rested his hand on the back of Morton's chair in a move that seemed natural. He pressed as hard as he could to stick the bug onto his jacket.

"No."

"But bullies, yeah. I'm really into video games and I don't go in for sports much so occasionally people try to make something of it."

"Ah, I can imagine. But you look like you could hold your own."

"I can if I have to," Jack said, turning back to his plate and pulling his hand back to pick up his knife.

"I'm sure you can, but if this boy becomes a problem to you then I want you to tell one of the staff, okay? We didn't invite you here to get picked on," Morton said and that seemed to be the end of the conversation.

The bug was in place. For a split second he felt a strong sense of pride at his first real spy work but it evaporated almost instantly. Morton's jacket was a dark colour and in this subdued light he couldn't see the bug but in daylight it might be far too obvious. Well, there was no going back now.

For the rest of the meal Morton spoke to other people and Jack did his best to make small talk with the guests around him. He just kept his head down and waited for it to end.

Once or twice Sauer made eye contact with him. Luckily they were too far apart to talk. It was probably Jack's imagination, but despite his overly friendly manner Jack was convinced the thin man disliked him.

When the meal finally drew to a close he stood with all of the others, but Morton placed a hand lightly on his arm.

"Can you wait behind please Jack?"

Jack swallowed, maybe he hadn't got away with it after all, maybe Morton just didn't want to ruin the dinner by drawing attention to it.

"Of course," he said.

He sat back down and noted nervously that Sauer hadn't moved either. It looked like whatever Morton wanted Jack for involved him as well.

Before long the others filed out and there was only Morton, Jack and Sauer left.

Morton looked at Jack and waved his hand towards his skeletal assistant.

"Sauer thinks you are a spy..." he said conversationally. Jack nearly choked but he did a better job of hiding his reaction this time and Morton carried on without noticing. "...For one of the big game companies."

Thank God! He doesn't really know at all.

Jack laughed and hoped it didn't sound as awkward as he felt.

"Sounds cool!" he said. "Do they give spy jobs to kids my age?"

"I don't imagine so," Morton said with a smile. "I told him that it was preposterous and I don't think he really believes it anyway, do you Sauer?" Sauer shrugged, making light of it but his eyes never left Jack and Jack could feel the hate boiling off him. Morton carried on, "But Jack, I wanted to reiterate that it is very important that you do not wander around outside of the GameZone here, okay?"

"Yes sir."

"And don't call me 'sir' Jack, it will make me feel old."

"No s... No, okay I won't. Is that all?"

Morton looked at Sauer who nodded his head very slightly.

"Yes, that's all. And if I don't see you again then enjoy the rest of your time here," Morton said.

"Thanks," Jack said, standing and smiling to both men nervously at the same time before he walked from the room as calmly as possible.

As soon as he was in the lift and the doors had closed behind him he slid down the wall to sit on the floor and catch his breath.

I am definitely not cut out for this, he thought.

CHAPTER TWELVE

Jack hurried to Abi's room as fast as he could. His mind played nasty tricks on him the whole way as he imagined all of the terrible things that must have happened to her.

If Sauer had caught her snooping around then Jack would never forgive himself.

He didn't know what he was doing involving her in the first place. People who had worked here were dead, this wasn't a game. Just because he felt alone and wanted someone to confide in didn't give him the right to put her in danger.

Jack had never been a particular fan of the law. He didn't feel he needed someone else to tell him what to do, but he did have a code of his own. He wouldn't do something he thought was wrong. And getting Abi caught was wrong.

By the time he reached her room he was running and was out of breath.

He looked around, conscious that people in the other rooms would hear him and if he was seen calling for her then they'd know they had been working together. He knocked lightly on the door and waited but there was no answer.

He knocked again, slightly louder this time but still she didn't come.

To hell with it, he thought. *I have to find out what's happened to her.*

"Abi!" he called and banged on the door. "Abi, are you in there?!"

He raised his fist again to hammer as hard as he could and the door shot open before his hand reached it. He stopped himself just in time to avoid hitting Abi in the face.

"What the hell are you doing?!" she asked angrily.

"You're okay!"

"Of course I'm okay. Is the building on fire?"

"What? No," he said. "I was worried about you. Can I come in?"

She looked unsure but she stood aside and let him in.

"What's going on Jack?" she asked registering that he was upset.

He garbled out the story.

"After we spoke I went back to my room and I got an invite to a meal with Morton. Didn't you?" he didn't give her chance to answer before running on, the words tumbling out of him. "I was scared they'd found out about me." He hesitated, he needed to remember that she didn't know everything. "About what I'd done I mean, with the bugs. And then I got there and the whole of Red Team were there so I thought it was okay but then you weren't and I panicked. I thought that..."

A look of understanding settled onto Abi's face.

"You thought something had happened to me."

"Yes."

"That's nice."

Jack caught himself. He hadn't wanted her to think of it as 'nice', he had just been worried about her. From the look in her eyes he was afraid she was getting the wrong idea.

"I mean, if you'd gone looking for anything. It was my fault. I don't care about you. I mean, I do care about you but... I just felt bad that was all."

Abi watched him with what looked like amusement on her face. She was older than him and it showed now.

"I'm okay," she said. "I got an invitation too but I couldn't make it. I felt ill."

"Oh. Right. Okay. Well, that's fine then. I'll leave you to it."

Jack turned to go but Abi grabbed his arm and stopped him.

"Not so fast you. You said you'd take me out tonight. You're still going out right?"

"I don't know," he said and meant it. *I thought she was dead. I really thought they'd killed her. I'm in over my head here.*

"Sure you are. Come on. It'll be exciting." She looked at her watch. "Go back to your room and calm down a bit then we'll meet like we said by the stairs."

"You feel well enough now?"

"What?"

"You said you were ill that's why you didn't go to Morton's meal."

"Oh, yes. I'm better now. I'll meet you there."

Jack lay awake on his bed until midnight. He had set an alarm to make sure he was awake in time and then tried to sleep but he couldn't stop his mind turning everything over.

Bobby.

Wallace.

Abi.

The Director.

Sauer's gaunt, evil-looking face.

Morton.

Bobby.

Bobby.

Bobby.

He had to do this. Eventually the clock showed that it was 12:00 and a second later his phone started to sound his alarm so he turned it off quickly before it disturbed anyone else.

He climbed off the bed, pulled his hood up and slunk out of his room. He got to the stairs without bumping into anyone. There was no way walking confidently would help him get away with this. If they were discovered then everything was over.

When he arrived there was no sight of Abi but he didn't panic, she probably just hadn't got there yet. He moved under the staircase into the shadows so he wasn't obvious if anybody should happen to come by and leant against the wall to wait for her.

A hand grabbed his shoulder from behind. He nearly screamed but just got a hold of himself in time and spun on the spot to see who had found him.

He looked up into Abi's grinning face. She looked like she was trying not to laugh as hard as he had tried not to scream.

"What are you doing hiding there?" he whispered harshly.

"Waiting for you. You're not really cut out for this spy stuff are you Jack?" she said, still grinning.

"I'm not a spy. I'm a reporter," he said guiltily.

She furrowed her eyebrows slightly.

"Are you annoyed with me?"

"No, no. You just... surprised me that's all."

"Surprised or scared?"

"Surprised," he insisted. "Now shall we get on with this?"

"Yes, sorry. You're the boss Jack, so what's the plan?"

"Well, I got a good look down here this morning and I didn't see anything obvious so I thought we'd start upstairs."

"Okay. Lead the way."

They crept out from underneath the stairs and headed up to the first floor. They went up the stairs in silence but when they reached the top Jack hesitated. He didn't really have a good plan at all.

"Should we look in every room?" Abi asked.

"I think we should, yes. We don't know exactly what we're looking for so let's check them all and see if we see anything odd."

The stairs ended at a long corridor lined with rooms and Jack and Abi worked their way along it slowly, the automatic lights turning on just ahead of them with every step they took.

Jack showed Abi how to plant the bugs and they had put one in every room. They had got half way down the corridor and found only meeting rooms. Jack didn't see how this was going to get CIRCLE what they needed. More likely they were going to get recordings of a bunch of boring meetings. The bugs he'd planted in the game zone probably wouldn't be any more use but at least they would be fun to listen to.

Jack hadn't expected spying to be so boring and Abi must have felt the same way because after a while the silence got to them and they started talking in hushed voices.

"So was the dinner any good then? Apart from being worried about me, I mean," Abi said mischievously.

"It was alright. I had to sit next to Simon Morton."

"You're kidding. That's amazing."

"Yes, I suppose it is really. I managed to get a bug onto his jacket."

"No way!"

"Yeah," he said. "He was asking me about Sebastien and I did it while we spoke."

"Wow. Maybe you are cut out for spying after all."

"Reporting," Jack said more sharply than he'd intended.

Abi raised her hands, "Just a joke."

They tried another few rooms without speaking and then Jack broke the silence.

"So what did you have to do to get picked by your school to come here?"

"Oh, I'm not representing a school. I got here the same way as Sebastien I'm afraid. I'm just somebody's daughter."

Jack froze with his hand on the next door handle and looked back at her.

"Wow, another president's kid. So is it your mum or your dad and where are they the president of?"

"Ha! Nothing like that." As she answered him Jack carelessly opened the door and looked inside expecting to see yet another meeting room or office. Behind him Abi continued to answer his question. "My dad works for the company..."

"Shh!" Jack interrupted her. "Get in here and look at this, quickly."

Jack pulled Abi inside the room and swept his arm around dramatically.

"What is this place?" he said.

"Oh my God, I don't know."

There was just enough light in the room to see by but it was dim, a low blue light like the sort that comes from a monitor rather than a proper light-bulb. It gave everything a sickly colour.

The room was organised like a hospital room. It was longer than the meeting rooms they had seen so far, perhaps taking up two or three of them and it was lined with beds.

All of the beds had someone lying in them.

Jack and Abi went to the nearest bed and looked at the person lying in it. Clipped to the foot of the bed was a chart with acronyms and numbers that Jack didn't understand. It didn't have a name on it but at the top, next to the word 'Subject' was a set of numbers that presumably identified the person in the bed.

There was a platform attached to the top of the bed. It stretched from one side to the other, about a foot above the subject's head and covered his face. The sickly blue light was coming from it.

Jack looked around and saw that all of the beds had one of the platforms. There was a hinge where it connected to the bed so Jack gingerly took hold of it and started to lift it.

Abi touched his arm.

"Should you do that?" she asked.

"I don't know but I want to see him."

Jack lifted the platform until it was pointing upwards. It wasn't a platform for resting things on at all. It was an LCD screen.

That explains the light, Jack thought. He leant forward to see the screen but it wasn't showing anything sensible, just a weird set of flashing lights.

"I, er... don't think you should look at that," Abi said.

"Why not?"

Jack looked at her, it seemed an odd thing to say but she just shrugged.

Her nerves must be getting to her, that's fair enough. I know how she feels.

She was obviously uncomfortable and there was nothing to learn by staring at the screen so Jack ignored it and studied the 'subject' instead.

He was a boy about Jack's age. His eyes were open but he didn't react to Jack at all. It was as though he was asleep with his eyes open. Jack had heard that was possible. When he'd been younger he had got a cut on his eyelid from a fight he'd been in and the next morning one of the carers at his home had said they'd come in and found him asleep with one eye stuck open. It had freaked her out but Jack hadn't known anything about it. He'd had a good night's sleep. So just because this boy's eyes were open didn't mean he was awake.

Jack lowered the platform screen back down and looked up the long room again.

"There must be thirty people here," he said to Abi. She nodded but said nothing. "Why would Morton Tech have patients?"

"I don't know, perhaps they're trying to help them?" she said, her voice quieter than before.

"They work for the Ministry of Defence, not the Health Service," he said thoughtfully, but he'd already moved on to the next bed.

Jack felt bad but he needed to know what was going on here, so he pulled back the blanket to see if there were any clues. Another boy. He was wearing a hospital gown but Jack couldn't see any injuries on his body. He went to cover him back up and then saw that his feet were secured to the bed by leather straps.

"What the...?! We need to tell somebody about this quickly. It can't be right."

"I think we need to find out more first," Abi said.

She was calm and she spoke normally, but it must have been too loud.

The patient in the bed two down from them started struggling and wriggled himself into position to sit up, pushing the screen out of his way with his body.

He looked to be about twenty and his eyes had the same wide open but empty look that the first boy had. His head flicked around manically but he made no sound.

Jack rushed to his side, Abi followed him reluctantly.

"Don't worry," Jack said. "It's alright. We're here to help."

The young man turned his head slowly towards Jack and Abi. He blinked and his vacant eyes focused briefly.

Then he screamed.

Jack looked at Abi.

"What do we do?" he asked urgently.

"I don't know. Comfort him?"

She reached forward and touched his arm but the young man only screamed louder.

"Here let me try."

Jack guessed that the man was having some sort of nightmare in which he thought Abi was someone else, so Jack took the man's face in both his hands and turned his eyes to his.

"It's alright," he said again, slowly and calmly. "We're going to get you some help."

The man stopped screaming and closed his eyes. Jack even felt some of the tension leave his body but he wouldn't lie back down however hard Jack pushed his shoulders. In the end he decided to leave him sitting up. At least he was calm.

"I don't like this at all," he said. "We need to finish up here quickly and get out. You find somewhere to put a couple of the bugs and I'll see if I can find anything that explains what's going on, then we're going back to our rooms. I've had enough of this."

"Okay," Abi whispered and looked relieved.

She headed back to the front of the room while Jack wandered the other way looking at the various charts on the patients' beds. None of them made any sense to him. He took a couple of pictures with his phone. He'd send them to CIRCLE when he got chance, they'd be able to work out what was going on.

He peered under another couple of monitors to look at the patients. They all looked well fed and cared for but every one of them had the same vacant look.

Suddenly Abi interrupted him.

"Jack! Listen, I think someone's coming!" she said in a shouted whisper.

Jack stood very still. Sure enough outside in the corridor there were footsteps approaching. He looked around for anywhere they could hide but the beds were all metal frames and the blankets went nowhere near the floor.

"What are we going to do?" Abi asked urgently. "Shall we tell them we got lost?"

"No, I've already said that today. They'll never believe me. We have to hide."

Jack and Abi watched from their hiding place as the door opened and two people stepped into the room in the middle of a conversation.

It was Sauer and a large woman who was wearing a white lab coat.

"It can't be nothing Doctor, why would the corridor lights be on? Somebody has been here," Sauer said.

His voice was harsh and accusing as though it was the doctor's fault. With nobody around to be falsely friendly to his manner was totally different. Jack thought that although it was unpleasant, this attitude fitted him better. Like seeing him in the suit instead of the hoodie. It was a more honest version of the man.

"I don't know sir. Perhaps there was a fault with the sensors."

"What is that subject doing sitting up?" Sauer demanded.

As soon as he spoke the man in the bed turned his head towards the sound. His eyes flicked open and he started screaming again. Sauer ignored the noise and continued to berate the doctor. "This project appears to be spinning out of control. You heard Mr Morton during the board meeting the other day. We cannot afford any more mistakes before the launch."

The big woman looked as though she wanted to argue but she had obviously learnt that it was pointless to disagree with Sauer.

"No sir," she said.

Sauer looked satisfied. He nodded and stepped back into the corner.

"I will wait here so nobody can get out. You start at the other end of the room and work your way up."

"Shouldn't Security be doing this, sir?"

"Are you questioning me Doctor? Do you want me to go and wake Mr Morton?"

"No, no, of course not. I'll go and check."

"Good. And for God's sake sedate that subject!" He pointed at the screaming man. The man's eyes had never left them and his screaming had grown louder.

The woman walked down the room with a rolling gait, glancing at the beds as she went. When she got to the bed with the screaming man she withdrew a syringe from the cupboard above his bed, filled it with something from a small bottle and injected it into his arm.

She was very matter of fact and didn't speak to him at all as she worked but she was not rough. Almost as soon as she took the needle out of his arm his face went slack and she gently lay him back in bed. Then she put his monitor back into place above his head and waddled to the far end of the room. When she reached the wall she turned and, hiding a sigh from Sauer, she started slowly heading back up to him looking under each of the beds in turn.

With every step she got closer and closer to Jack and Abi.

A minute earlier, with the footsteps coming down the corridor towards the room, Jack had thought lightning fast about where to hide.

"How much do you weigh?" he asked Abi.

"What?!"

"How much do you weigh? Quickly. "

"I don't know exactly. About eight and a half stone."

Jack did some mental maths. It was very borderline but it should work if they didn't move. He yanked his bag from his shoulder and dug around inside to find the gecko gloves Alice had given him. He got hold of them, straightened up, grabbed Abi and broke into a sprint towards the door, tugging her along with him.

"We can't go out that way, they'll see us!" Abi said.

"We're not going out. We're going up," he said, pulling his gloves on. "Put your arms around my neck and hold on tight."

Abi did as he asked and grabbed onto him. She was a little bit taller than him so it wasn't easy but he shuffled his way up the wall, one hand and one foot on either side of the corner.

"How are you doing this?" Abi asked as Jack clambered like an ungainly Spiderman up the wall.

"Spe...cial... shoes and... gloves..." Jack panted.

They reached the ceiling and Jack pressed Abi back against the wall then braced himself in place across the corner. He could feel the gloves straining to take their combined weight so he pushed his hands and feet as hard as he could into the walls to stop them from slipping. "I'm going to try to hold us here," he said when he could speak again. "Don't move at all or they'll stop working."

A second later the door swung open and hit the wall beneath them. It missed Abi's feet by less than a centimetre and she pulled them up quickly.

The gloves loosened slightly as she moved and Jack's eyes went wide. He couldn't speak but he shook his head at her a tiny fraction and hoped she understood. She buried her face into his shoulder and he guessed that she had.

He clung on for dear life and prayed the gloves would hold.

The doctor walked up the room checking under every bed as she went. Every time she raised her head Jack was afraid she'd look just a little bit higher and see them pressed against the ceiling like a giant fly. There would be no way to explain what they were doing here now that they had tried to hide.

He and Abi stayed as still as they possibly could.

If Jack was afraid that the doctor would spot them then he was *absolutely terrified* that Sauer would.

The skeletal assistant was standing directly beneath them and Jack's mind was tormented with images of him hearing them, or smelling the sweat that was beading on Jack's forehead even now, and turning his skull-like head to look at them.

The doctor was grumbling as she went but annoyingly she was doing a very thorough job.

Hurry up! Jack thought, feeling the gloves start to slip. The best way to get a better grip was to lift his hands off one at a time and plant them on again but he daren't do that. If he moved any of his hands or feet he was afraid they'd give out and they'd both fall. And the bony Sauer would do nothing to break their fall.

After what felt like a year she reached the man who had been screaming.

"Is this entirely necessary?" she called to Sauer. "If there had been anyone in here they would have run out as we came in surely. Nobody would be stupid enough to try hiding in here."

Jack resisted the urge to nod in agreement. He didn't think the gloves could stand the movement.

"Someone has been here Doctor," Sauer said.

"We don't know that. The lights might have come on because of the screamer."

She was checking fairly quickly under each bed now as they spoke. Just bending slightly and half looking while she waved her leg under it.

"So what disturbed him then?"

"I don't know," the doctor said as she finished checking the last bed and finally reached Sauer. "But whatever it was, it wasn't an intruder. Now can I go back to my bed, please?"

Sauer hesitated. Jack nearly cried out from the pain in his muscles and the terror in his head. Eventually he answered her.

"Very well," he said, threw the door open and stalked out. As soon as he was out of sight the doctor rolled her eyes and shook her head dramatically and then, to Jack's relief, she followed him from the room.

As soon as Sauer and the doctor had left the room, Jack climbed down as quickly as he possibly could.

He and Abi decided they'd taken enough chances that night and that they needed to get back to their rooms as quickly as they could before anyone noticed they were missing. They hurried quietly through the corridors straight back to their rooms, only speaking when Jack left Abi at the door to her room.

They exchanged a look and Abi broke the silence.

"Talk in the morning?" she asked quickly.

Jack nodded but didn't reply. He waited until she opened her door and then ran as fast as he could back to his room. Some sixth sense was nagging at the back of his head and convinced him he still wasn't in the clear.

He reached his room and dived straight into bed fully clothed and pulled the covers up to his chin just like he had when he was a little boy and had been afraid of monsters in his room.

He had just enough time to notice how much his muscles ached and start to feel stupid when, less than a minute after he had got into bed, he heard the door to his room open slightly.

Jack lay very still and breathed deeply. He didn't trust himself to fake a snore but he had seen plenty of other people sleep and he knew that even when they weren't snoring they had a deep regular breathing. He did his best to copy it now.

As he lay there, a light swept over his face as whoever was at the door shone a torch into the room. He kept his eyes closed but mumbled as though he was disturbed.

A second later the door closed again quietly and Jack heard the distinctive footsteps he'd come to recognise move away.

Sauer! he thought. *Holy crap, that was close.*

He felt a strange mix of triumph and fear. Fear because he knew beyond doubt that Sauer definitely suspected him and triumph because he knew for sure now that there was definitely something going on here.

Now if only I knew what it was, he thought.

CHAPTER THIRTEEN

The next morning Jack had some welcome relief from the world of espionage. It was the first day of the GamesCon convention and the beta testers were going to be putting on a demonstration of Shark for the assembled VIPs.

He felt guilty for losing himself back into gaming but he thought he'd done enough for CIRCLE over the last couple of days. Their analysts could use the time to study if the bugs he'd planted had found anything. When he had woken up he had found that they had sent him a message through the SWAT Team IV message board overnight arranging to meet him in the convention hall this evening, but until then he did not intend to give them another thought. He was owed a bit of a rest. And whatever other evil stuff Morton Tech might be doing they had definitely made a brilliant gaming platform in Shark.

GamesCon was a two day event that brought the gaming world together. Big companies used it to release their new games so that they could make the biggest splash possible. And all of the most famous people in the gaming world came.

This year Morton Tech was hosting it as part of their plan to launch Shark.

Jack had followed GamesCon for the last three years but he had never thought he would actually go to one. He would never have been able to afford tickets. Now he wasn't just going, he was standing on stage. Imagine what Frank would think when he saw it, he'd go mental.

Oh damn, he thought. *Is that a problem? If they mention my name Frank will know it isn't real.*

He was in the GameZone with Abi and about half of the other beta testers. They were standing in loose little groups and Sauer, Sandra and Alex were working their way through them all, fitting them with packs like you might wear in a game of laser tag and checking that their glasses would broadcast their in-game view up to the big screens for the audience to see.

When Sandra bustled past him with a handful of packs for the Blue Team, Jack put his hand out to stop her.

"Yes Jack?"

"Erm... are we going to be on TV?"

"Not mainstream TV but GamesCon are streaming it on their official channel and Morton Tech will post some highlights after the formal launch tomorrow. And of course lots of the guests are YouTubers, you can bet they'll be recording it. Isn't that cool?"

"Yeah, cool," Jack said. *Great, another problem,* he thought. Well this was one that CIRCLE would have to sort out, he'd tell them and let them worry about it. He couldn't fix everything. They'd put him here.

Abi sensed his reluctance and when Sandra had bustled off she frowned.

"Don't you want to be on telly?" she asked.

"I'm not bothered either way," Jack said. He felt bad keeping the truth from her but he couldn't explain it without telling her too much.

At that moment Sauer, a pack over each arm, interrupted. Jack had never been more pleased to see him, which wasn't saying much, of course.

He placed the pack in his right hand on the floor and waved the left hand pack in front of Jack.

"Your pack Mr Dawson!" he said with his usual forced cheeriness. "We need to get you all suited up! Raise your arms please."

Jack did as he said and Sauer dropped a pack over his arms and down onto his shoulders. Then he moved round to Jack's back and tightened the pack like he was putting a corset on a Victorian lady. A lady who needed a peculiarly tight corset.

"Does it need to be that tight?" Jack asked, his voice distorted by his inability to breathe out fully.

"We don't want it to come off in the game."

"Do we want me to be able to breathe in the game?"

Sauer shook his head as though Jack had deeply disappointed him and relaxed the pack a tiny bit.

"Better?" he asked.

"Yes, thank you."

Sauer took a step sidewards to Abi.

"And yours."

Abi went through the same process but he was evidently more careful when tightening hers as she didn't complain.

When he was finished he looked at them both and then gave an oddly formal little nod of his head that could almost have been a bow.

"Mr Dawson. Abi," he said and then withdrew.

When he was safely out of earshot Jack pulled a face at his retreating back.

"He gives me the creeps," he said to Abi. He kept his voice quiet even though the man was on the other side of the room now, perching by the table with the packs and letting Sandra and Alex do the rest of the work.

Two minutes later everyone had a pack on and Sandra gathered them all together.

"Okay people, we all know why we're here. The full launch of Shark will take place tomorrow. There will be a crowd of some really quite important people there from the political realm. Including even Madame Lefevre, the president of France," she said with a smile and a nod towards Sebastien. Most of the heads turned to look at him and he nodded happily like he'd got some sort of praise.

Yeah, well done on your hard work being born, Jack thought sarcastically, but he kept his thoughts to himself.

Sandra carried on unaware of Jack's mental commentary, "But before that Morton Tech wants to build up the buzz and excitement in the gaming community. In the end it's what people like you think that really matters, not a bunch of stuffy politicians, right?" This time the crowd of beta testers cheered. Jack smiled and noticed that Sebastien stopped at exactly the same time. "So we're going to go out there and show them why it is you've fallen in love with Shark since you've been here. We'll play in here as normal but the feed from your glasses will be broadcast out to the audience live. The game we'll be playing is called Terrorist Hunt. When we start the game one of the older players will be randomly assigned to be the terrorist. If that's you then your glasses will tell you. Your job is simply to get away and survive for three minutes, if you do that then you will have won and the 'bomb' will go off. The rest of you have to find the terrorist and take them down. At the start of the game your glasses will show you an image of the terrorist and make whoever has been chosen look like them."

"Why the packs Sandra?" asked a tester Jack recognised from the blue team.

Sandra shot Sauer a sideways look but he didn't look like he was going to speak so she answered the question herself.

"Well, we want to put on an interesting show right?"

"Yeah."

"Well the audience screens will cycle through the view that your glasses are showing you but they won't get the same sense of excitement that you all get from being in the game. So Morton Technology wanted to introduce an edge..." She hesitated as though uncertain or perhaps even unhappy with what she was going to say next. "So the packs deliver an electric shock."

"An electric shock?!"

"It's perfectly harmless," she said hurriedly.

"Hurts like buggery though," said Alex.

She looked at him and then reluctantly nodded. "Yes. It does. Do you want to explain any further Dr Sauer?" She looked meaningfully at Sauer but Sauer just shrugged.

"No, I think you're doing a fine job Sandra."

Jack got the distinct feeling that Sandra had only just learnt of the shock packs. That Sauer, or maybe even Morton, had made the decision and left her to deliver the bad news. He wondered what she'd done to annoy them. Maybe they just enjoyed tormenting people.

Sandra paused slightly, surprised by the lack of help from Sauer but then she recovered and carried on.

"So if you're the terrorist, you're really going to want to survive to the end because your pack will give you an electric shock each time any of the other players get you in their sights. If they land a shot on you then the shock will be doubled and the game will end. That's why the terrorist has to be over eighteen. Under eighteens have a pack that only gives one level of shock. And it's much smaller."

"And if you're not the terrorist?" This time it was a red team member that asked the question.

"If the terrorist shoots you then you get the same as he or she would. But if you don't capture the terrorist before the end of the game and the 'bomb' goes off then all of the hunters get shocked. The idea is that it will help raise the stakes for the audience."

There were some concerned looks shared between the testers but nobody wanted to be the one to argue. Particularly as they were about to go on stage in one of the biggest events of the year.

Jack looked across at Abi but she wasn't reacting. He tried to take the same approach. He could handle a little electric shock. He could even understand how the threat would ramp up the adrenaline for the crowd. He was glad he couldn't be the terrorist though, it didn't sound like a lot of fun.

"Any other questions?" Sandra asked.

Nobody spoke.

"Okay, if you're all good to go let's do it. Take your positions."

The testers filed out to the sides to wait for the announcer to finish introducing the game.

When it was Jack's turn to pass Sauer, the corpse-like man leant forward and winked a papery thin eyelid over his eye.

"Enjoy the game Mr Dawson," he said and grinned making him look even more like a skull.

Jack got a sinking feeling in his stomach that somehow he knew about last night.

He might suspect but he can't know anything for sure, he thought and tried to put it from his mind and concentrate on the game. This was going to be fun.

Jack crouched in one of his favourite spots in the zone and waited for the game to begin. He and Abi had split up, deciding it was better that they weren't together too much because it might draw attention.

Not long after he had chosen his position his Shark glasses had started showing a little countdown in the top right corner that told him how long until the game started.

The announcer droned on and Jack shuffled uncomfortably. His pack was still too tight, bloody Sauer.

3...

2...

1...

The world his glasses showed him changed as Shark drew the game world of Terrorist Hunt over the top of the real one.

This is it, he thought excitedly. *I get to play the world's most exciting new game live on stage at GamesCon! Perhaps life as a spy isn't so bad after all.*

A small window opened in the bottom left of his field of vision showing him a video feed of the crowd. They'd never done that before but then they'd never played in front of a crowd before. He guessed it was so the players could see the reaction of the audience. There was a little icon indicating that he could dismiss it if he wanted but he left it for now while he explored what else Terrorist Hunt had to offer.

The scenery of the GameZone had been changed into the world of the hunt, but this one wasn't taking place in a magical forest. It was a bombed out city. There were cars and half demolished buildings. He smiled to himself, it was quite similar to SWAT Team IV.

Finally, a character card appeared floating in the foreground that told him who his character in the game was. The rules of this game weren't complicated and he didn't care too much what part he was playing. The way Sandra had described it the only character that had a different role to play was the terrorist and that couldn't be him because he wasn't old enough. He gave the card a casual glance and went to dismiss it. Then he froze in horror.

That can't be right!

The card said he was the terrorist.

The picture was of a middle aged man with a beard, long dirty blond hair and an AK47 gun held casually in his hands. And across the picture the word WANTED was stamped in red ink.

There must be some sort of mistake, he thought. Then he heard the sound of running feet approaching and turned to his right just in time to see someone duck behind a wall.

Still dumbfounded by the fact that he was the terrorist he kept looking stupidly in that direction and saw when the other player stepped out and locked his sights onto Jack.

Almost instantaneously a powerful electric shock ran through Jack's body.

"Argh!" he screamed as his body convulsed.

His scream was more from shock than pain but it hurt enough to confirm what the character card had told him. He was the terrorist. Mistake or not he had to get moving.

He dropped to the floor and commando crawled away out of sight of the other player. Once he was round the nearest wall he stood up and ran. He had only got twenty feet away when his gaming instincts kicked in and he regretted it instantly, if this had been SWAT Team IV he'd have waited by the corner for the other player to chase him and killed him as he turned it. The adrenaline that the shock had released was making it hard to think. He forced himself to stop running and walk back to the corner, gun raised.

The other player took longer than he expected to round the corner and the idea of experiencing real pain made keeping his position harder than in any game he'd ever played. But he held his nerve and waited.

Sure enough, the other player peeped round the wall. They weren't stupid enough to run blindly round a corner so whichever player it was wasn't bad, but Jack was better. He had his gun trained on the wall at head height and, as soon as he got a glimpse of them, he fired.

The shot landed and a counter at the top of his vision changed from '37 vs. 1' to '36 vs.1'

Great, he thought, sarcastically. *Just thirty six more of them to kill and it's all over.*

He knew without being arrogant that he was very good at SWAT Team IV and this was similar enough that he figured he'd be good at it too, but nobody was good enough to beat thirty six other players. He was going to get slaughtered.

He wondered if there was a way for the terrorist to give up but Sandra hadn't mentioned one and he couldn't do it even if there was. If he gave up then Morton Tech wouldn't get their show for GamesCon and they'd probably send him home. And if they sent him home then CIRCLE wouldn't help Bobby. There was only one thing for it. He had to keep playing and just hope either no-one else found him or he got killed quickly.

He shook his head.

Today was supposed to be fun, he thought.

Jack's plan was to hide from all of the other players and let the game timeout. There was no way he could possibly win by taking them all on.

He spotted a wrecked petrol station on the outskirts of the game area and made a break for it, dodging from cover to cover. He was only spotted by three players, but two of them managed to get him in their sights and shock him. The shocks were not pleasant but after the surprise of the first one had worn off the pain was not actually that bad. As long as he didn't let any of them shoot him he figured he would be fine.

Finally he made it to the petrol station and ducked backwards through the broken doorway so he could check no-one had followed him. He had a good view from here of the open ground in front of the station so he would know if anyone was coming.

He checked the timer in his glasses. He only had to last two more minutes and then the game would be over. Relief washed over him. It might not make for very good viewing for the audience but at least he would avoid being shot. He didn't fancy getting a shock twice as powerful as the ones he had already had.

His relief did not last long.

"Bad luck friend," came a voice from behind him and Jack's heart sank.

He turned just in time to see that a group of three hunters had obviously had the very same idea he had and had waited here to ambush the terrorist. Him.

All three of them opened fire at the same time. Jack did not even have time to raise his gun.

The shock that went through Jack's body was excruciating. He fell instantly to the floor, his body shaking and writhing.

When it finally stopped pulsing through him and the pain subsided Jack felt curiously pleased.

At least it's over now, he thought and struggled to his knees, hands raised.

The hunters obviously thought the same thing as they stopped firing and two of them raised their glasses onto the top of their heads.

Then two very bad things happened at the same time.

Jack saw that the timer in his glasses had not stopped and one of the hunters spoke.

"Well, well, well, look who it is. It's little Jackie."

Jack recognised the accent at the same time that he saw the timer was still counting. Sebastien.

The French boy raised his gun again and pointed it at Jack threateningly.

"Pity it's over," he said.

"It isn't," said the hunter who had left his glasses on, sounding puzzled. "He's not dead."

"What do you mean?" Sebastien asked.

"Just that. The game thinks he still alive. We must have missed. I'll take him."

"No! I want him!" Sebastien said but the other boy had already fired at Jack.

The same incredibly powerful shock coursed through Jack's body again sending him back onto the floor.

"It's not working. He is still alive," the other boy said. His voice had no sympathy in it, he might have been studying an insect.

Sebastien grinned and lowered his glasses.

One minute he saw Jack squirming on the floor, the next, with his glasses down it was the terrorist.

"Oh dear. Poor Jackie. It looks like the game doesn't want you to die. I wonder how many shots you can take before you lose control and wet yourself."

Jack braced himself. It was worse now that he knew what was coming.

Sebastien opened fire and the shot rang out.

Ten seconds later the wave of pain finished and Jack could think again, just about. He'd been shot three times now and his mind was getting fuzzier each time the pack delivered its maximum shock. He didn't know how long he could possibly hold out. Or what would happen when he couldn't. He wanted to be dead but he knew he wouldn't die from an electric shock. Just be in agony.

Sebastien knew the same thing. And he had an excuse to release his inner bully.

He kept shooting.

Jack didn't want to beg but in the end he couldn't stop himself.

"Stop! Please!" he cried.

Sebastien laughed and shot him again.

Jack couldn't focus on the timer but he knew there couldn't be long left.

The shocks felt like they lasted forever, in reality it was only about ten seconds but each time he stopped shaking Sebastien shot him again. Through the haze of pain he heard Sebastien and his friends talking. He couldn't understand what they were saying but from the tone of their voices it sounded like the other hunters were telling Sebastien to stop. But he wouldn't.

His mind a jumble, Jack kept shaking. He thought that he might have decided that if he kept shaking Sebastien would stop but he couldn't be sure if he really had decided it or if he had just lost control of his body.

His last thought before he blacked out from the pain was that Sebastien might have been right about him wetting himself.

He hoped not.

CHAPTER FOURTEEN

When he woke up it felt like an age had passed but it couldn't have been more than a minute.

Sandra was leaning over him with her hand on his shoulder.

"Jack, I'm so sorry. This shouldn't have happened."

Jack looked up at her and then rested his head back onto the floor. There was a pool of drool and tears where he had been lying but he was grateful that was all there was.

With the pain removed Jack's mind was back to normal. All that was left was the embarrassment at lying on the floor surrounded by the testers. Again.

All of the testers and support staff had gathered around. He guessed that they'd finished the game and closed down the audience link at some point while he was being shot. Most of the testers were standing near him, looking down with various degrees of concern but in the background Jack saw Sebastien talking to a small group of his own. Sauer was with him listening with a worried look on his skull like face.

"We thought the terrorist was supposed to be older," Sebastien was saying. "We did not know it was him."

"Of course not! I hope you can forgive Morton Tech for this unfortunate incident, Mr Lefevre," Sauer said, laying a hand on Sebastien as if he was the one who had been shocked.

Sandra leant forward and spoke again.

"I don't know how it happened Jack. The terrorist was supposed to be an adult. And the game should have cut out when you got shot the first time. I'll look into it."

Sauer broke off from Sebastien's fan club and strode over, his shoes clacking against the floor and stood behind Sandra, looming over her and looking down on Jack.

"Oh come now! Let's not make too much of this. The pack cannot harm you unless you have a heart condition which we know Jack does not. It is just a little pain, he is fine, aren't you Jack?!" He narrowed his eyes at Jack and the corner of his mouth lifted a fraction. It was very small but it was unmistakable. He wanted Jack to know it had been him.

But was it because he knows what I saw last night? Or just because I embarrassed him in front of Morton?

Jack looked away, too shaken up to engage in a battle of wills with this man.

"Yes, I'm fine," he muttered. He felt like a coward but he didn't have any fight left in him right now.

"Quite!" Sauer turned and addressed the group, his usual fake cheerfulness amplified. "Anyway, the important thing is the demonstration was a success! The crowd loved Shark! Well done all of you. Now if you'll clean this up Sandra, I'm going to go out on stage."

Without waiting for Sandra to reply he stalked off.

The crowd started drifting away but Sandra stayed where she was and smiled kindly at Jack.

"Are you really alright?"

"I will be," he said. "Like he said, it's just pain, right?"

Jack righted his glasses on his face automatically and sure enough he could see that Sauer was right about the crowd loving Shark. The crowd were going wild, of course, they were completely unaware that the 'terrorist' had been a child. Not that Jack knew whether it would have changed their mind anyway.

Abi took Jack out into the crowd an hour later to watch the rest of GamesCon as a member of the audience.

His body had totally recovered now and he was half annoyed to see that Sauer had been right about the shocks. They hadn't had any lasting effect on him at all.

He and Abi talked quietly as they wandered from stand to stand, drinking too much coke and eating giant bags of popcorn because, as Shark Beta Testers, they had passes that meant they got them for free.

When they were in the middle of the room, surrounded by normal guests who didn't know them, he took the chance to say something that had occurred to him while Sauer was smirking down at him in the GameZone.

"I've been thinking, what if Morton isn't really in charge?"

Abi stopped walking and looked at him carefully.

"What makes you say that?"

He gave her arm a tug to get them moving again so they didn't look out of place and carried on in a quiet voice.

"Well, he's a bit weird, maybe even a bit spaced out, but he doesn't strike me as the evil genius type."

"And you think there's an evil genius here?" Abi said, watching him over the top of her drink as she took a big gulp.

"Okay, maybe evil is a bit strong but like we said, something's going on. I think maybe Sauer is in charge."

Abi's eyes bugged out and she nearly choked on her drink.

She managed to avoid spitting it all over him but it took a minute for her coughing to subside.

When she'd finished she answered him.

"You just think that because he's... cruel."

"He got me electrocuted," Jack said. Abi raised an eyebrow at him and he qualified it. "You know what I mean. He certainly got me hurt badly on purpose."

"We don't know that. But anyway, no, I don't think he's in charge. I think Simon Morton is. He's the CEO."

She seemed very sure so he dropped it but he wasn't convinced. He filed away the thought to pass along to CIRCLE and they carried on wandering around the various exhibits, trying out a few of the newest games together. Jack was much better than Abi, she claimed that was because normal games were designed for boys and therefore were too easy for people of her intelligence.

"Girls, you mean?!"

"You said it."

"Unbelievable!" He laughed. In truth he was just glad to see that the electric shocks hadn't upset his gaming skills and to be a normal fourteen year old for a while.

He checked his watch. There was still another hour before he was supposed to meet CIRCLE. He could afford to enjoy himself.

"Let's go and see the Shark display," he said.

Abi wasn't keen.

"Why bother?" she said. "We already know what they'll be showing. Sandra told us it's a replay of the game from earlier and a Q&A session. Do you want to listen to a bunch of people who know less about Shark than we do?"

"Well, I need a sit down and they're on the main stage. Let's go and grab a seat before it starts."

"If you just want to sit down we could go back to the GameZone or the restaurant. Or even one of our rooms. Somewhere without all of these people."

"Are you okay?" he frowned.

"Yeah, I just don't want you to get upset watching the game."

"I won't get upset."

He pulled her along and she went reluctantly.

Jack sent her inside to find a seat and went to get them both another drink. When he came back, laden down with as much as he could carry, he spotted her in the raised bank of seats at the back of the hall.

He clumsily handed her a drink, freeing one of his hands at last.

"What are you doing way back here? We can hardly see the stage at all."

"We can see well enough."

"Come on," he said and grabbed her hand and pulled her closer to the front without letting her argue.

He chose seats about mid-way down the hall, which was as close to the stage as they could get, and arranged all of their drinks and snacks around them. After a while the lights went down and an announcer started doing a countdown in the excited 'voiceover guy' voice.

Spotlights tumbled around the stage and then focused onto a group of players who came onto the stage wearing silver jumpsuits and Shark glasses. Their movements were perfectly in time making them look eerily like synchronised swimmers but on dry land.

Cool! They look like robots in those suits, he thought. And the Shark glasses completed the look. They spilled a blue light out onto the players' faces from whatever changes the screens were making to the world.

There was something familiar about them but he didn't recognise any of them from the GameZone.

128

"Who are they, do you know?" he asked Abi in a hushed voice.

Abi hesitated and shuffled in her seat, presumably to get a closer look at them.

"I think they're the Elites. The testers who got promoted before you arrived."

"Oh nice one. This could be good then. Do you think they're going to play another live game after all?" He was gradually forgetting his upset from earlier and settling into enjoying the GamesCon as he'd planned that morning.

"I don't know any more than you do Jack," Abi replied with an edge.

Jeez, take a breath. It's not you who got zapped by enough electricity to curl your hair, he thought but he rolled his eyes and decided to ignore her. Whatever was eating her, it was her problem. He intended to enjoy this.

He turned back to the stage and watched as the Elites took up places behind the announcers. Their jumpsuits would be perfect for a game but if they were going to play something then it obviously wasn't going to be Terrorist Hunt because none of them had a shock-pack on.

He watched them to see if he could get any clue as to what they were about to demonstrate. He hoped it was another game. He'd never got to watch a Shark game from outside. It'd be good to know what it was like. He didn't expect CIRCLE to let him keep a set of glasses when this was all over and he certainly wouldn't be able to afford one, so he'd probably be a spectator for a while. He might as well get used to it.

But none of the Elites seemed about to do anything interesting and now that he thought about it there wouldn't really be enough room for any of the good games on that stage. He guessed they were just there to make Morton look cool. Well, it was working.

He tuned the announcer out and imagined himself up there with them.

And then it hit him all at once.

He did recognise them.

At least one of them.

The guy second in from the right was definitely the screamer from last night. And he was pretty sure that the others had been there too.

The sickly blue light that was coming from their glasses was exactly the same as the light from the monitors in the room last night.

It was all connected.

The weird deaths, the reason CIRCLE had sent him, Shark, the room with the vacant staring people.

All of it.

And the reason they looked like robots was because they basically were. Human robots.

Wallace and the Director had thought Shark was just a good excuse for him to get inside Morton Tech but it wasn't a coincidence. It was the problem.

Someone was controlling these people's minds through Shark. Why hadn't he seen it before?!

He opened his mouth to tell Abi and then stopped himself just in time. He couldn't drag her any further into it now. This was much worse than just planting some bugs. He had to tell CIRCLE. He checked his watch. Twenty minutes until they were supposed to make contact with him.

He couldn't just wait here though. He had to try to find them. They needed to see this.

He stood up.

"Where are you going?" Abi asked, looking up at him.

"I've got to... I need the loo. You stay here."

She looked confused but shrugged and turned back to the stage.

As he left the hall he looked back over at her, desperately sorry for having dragged her into this. She was looking in his direction at the same time and for a moment they made eye contact. He smiled at her and ran from the hall.

CHAPTER FIFTEEN

Jack ran from the hall filled with a sense of purpose. He had to tell CIRCLE what he knew.

As soon as he was outside the main hall and saw the number of people in the convention, his shoulders sagged.

At first he walked around the convention with determined steps. He wasn't running but he was definitely striding. After a couple of minutes the ridiculousness of his chances struck him and his steps slowed.

How am I supposed to find them in here? He assumed they wouldn't come without some sort of disguise but he had no idea what it would be.

The plan was for them to meet him in twenty minutes so they must be here somewhere. For that matter, now he thought about it they hadn't told him how they would find him either. They hadn't agreed a meeting place, just told him a time and to be on his own. He had just assumed they would handle it.

He kept circling the centre, eyes darting all over the crowd trying to pick out a face he recognised, then it occurred to him that they might not even send anyone he knew. He had expected it to be Wallace but they wouldn't necessarily send him. They must have thousands of agents.

He was about to give up hope and wait for them to get in contact with him when he bumped into a man in a battledroid costume from Solar Empire.

"Sorry," Jack started to say absentmindedly then looked at the man. Oh no, he'd spilt his drink all down his front. "Oh no, I really am sorry. Can I help? I can get you another drink."

The droid stared at him.

"I don't want another drink. I need to get this one out of my joints. I'll be stuck in here forever if I don't. Can you help me?"

Jack wanted to say no. He could hardly spare the time but how was he supposed to do that? The man was very obviously annoyed.

"Look at me!" the man said and knocked his chest plate with his metal hands making a ringing sound. Jack followed the sound and then had to stifle a smile. The serial number printed on the droid's chest, exactly where the man had banged his hands in pretend outrage, was JH3101. Jack's real initials and birthday.

"Yes, of course. I really am very sorry. Where can we go to clean you up?" he said.

"Well I don't want to get out of this costume in the open do I?! Where's the nearest bathroom?"

"This way," Jack said and led the dripping droid to the toilet trailing a set of wet footprints.

When they were in the bathroom Jack checked if there was anyone in the stalls. Luckily there wasn't.

"We're alone," he said.

"Thank God, I can barely move in this thing," came a normal voice that Jack recognised. The droid lifted its head off and Wallace grinned at him. "Hang on, let me just get us some privacy."

He opened his chest plate and produced a small door wedge and a sign that read 'Out of Order'. He opened the door a fraction and slipped the sign over the handle outside, then closed it and pushed the wedge firmly under the bottom of the door.

"It's not as good as a lock but unless someone really forces it we'll be fine."

"Agent W..." Jack began but Wallace raised a hand to stop him and pulled a third thing from his chest plate.

It was a small black box with a switch and two lights on it. He turned it on and both lights came on, a red one and a green one. A second later the red one flicked off and Wallace started sweeping his arm about the room. The green light stayed on the whole time.

When he'd finished he leant casually on one of the sinks, looked at Jack and smiled.

"Bug sweeper. Always assume you're being overheard, son, until you prove otherwise. And never use names anyway."

Jack nodded, he really was out of his depth here.

"I'm so glad to see you." Wallace raised an eyebrow, surprised at the passion Jack spoke with. Jack was surprised as well but the relief he felt at not being alone was huge. "I know what they're doing."

Wallace came alert.

"What?"

"It's Shark, it's some sort of mind control."

"Shark?"

"The game!" Jack said in frustration. How could he not know what it was?! But then like Jack had thought earlier, Shark really wasn't on CIRCLE's radar. They thought whatever was going on here was connected to Morton's work on defence.

To his credit though, Wallace reacted quickly.

"Of course, okay, I remember. But really? How do you know?"

Jack explained about his exploring the night before, the room with the patients in and the strange blue light, the Shark glasses and above all how Sauer had known all about it.

"So you think it's him. You think Sauer is running the show," Wallace asked.

"I don't know to be honest. Abi thinks that just because he's a nasty piece of work it doesn't mean he's in charge."

Wallace frowned and stood up straight.

"Abi? Who's Abi and why does she know anything about this?"

Jack waved his hands dismissively but he caught the tone in Wallace's voice and wondered again if he'd gone too far getting her involved at all.

"She's one of the testers but you don't need to worry about her. She thinks something is going on here as well."

"This really isn't good, son. The plan was for you to do this alone. What have you told her?"

"Nothing about CI... Nothing about you. Or about me, really. I told her I wanted to be a reporter when I grow up and I was doing a story on Morton."

"Alright. That's not too bad. What's her full name? I'll look into her," Wallace asked.

Jack felt stupid. He didn't know. Some spy he was, he didn't even know Abi's surname. Wallace saw it in his face and seemed genuinely worried but he put it aside for now.

"Okay, look, don't worry about it. Her name's Abi and she's one of the testers, I'll do some digging. I'm sure you've handled it fine. It's difficult being in the field on your own for the first time. I understand. Forget that for now. We've got bigger fish to fry. Before it died, one of the bugs you planted on Morton indicated that something is going to happen tomorrow."

"That's the official launch date of Shark."

"I can't believe we didn't connect it." Wallace shook his head.

"You just thought it was a game. It's not really your sort of thing," Jack said comfortingly, their roles reversed for a minute.

Wallace looked at him thoughtfully.

"No, that's true, but you spotted it. Well done."

"Thank you," Jack said and meant it. Not very many people had praised Jack in his life so far and when they had it was usually just as an introduction to an insult or a criticism. 'Jack is a bright boy *but*...'; 'Jack has lots of potential *but*...'

Wallace brushed it off and got back to business.

"Blimey, mind control. That's massive. So have you been able to get any idea what they're planning to do with it?"

"No. But if they can make people kill themselves like on that video you showed me then they can do just about anything they want." Jack thought about everything he'd seen but couldn't come up with any more clues. "Haven't your people got anything else from my bugs?"

"I'm afraid not," Wallace said. Jack looked disappointed but Wallace went on quickly, "That's just the way of it with bugs. Most of them don't provide anything useful. The really good ones on Morton and in his room died really quickly. He must have found them. We were lucky to pick up the fact about tomorrow."

They were both silent for a minute and then Jack sighed.

"Well I guess I'll just have to keep looking then," he said.

Wallace shook his head.

"I don't think that's a good idea. Whether it's Sauer or Morton who's in charge, this is bad. It's time we got you out."

"No! I mean, I want to get out. I'm no good at this and, to be honest, I'm scared. But I haven't given you what you need. And if I don't then the Director won't help my... you know." He meant Bobby and Wallace knew it.

"Son. I don't want you to worry about that. I'll put in a word for you. This is getting dangerous. It's no place for a child."

Jack bristled, he didn't like being patronised even if it was in his best interest. Besides, he knew the right thing to do and he intended to do it.

"Even if you do... even if they help him... there's still something bad going to happen here and we don't know what it is, do we?"

Wallace shook his head, reluctant to admit the truth. "No."

"And you need to know what their plan is before you can stop it," Jack said and waited for Wallace to nod his agreement. "But you can't get anyone else in here quickly enough to do that can you?"

"No, we can't."

"So it's got to be me, hasn't it?"

Wallace fought against it briefly. Jack saw the decision on his face when he gave in.

"Okay," he said. "But we're going to keep working on it outside as well. I want you to keep an eye on the message board and if we find anything that means you don't need to be here we'll post it up there. If you see that then you get out fast."

"I will."

"And don't do anything stupid. Your job is only to find out what's going on. I'm going to be putting a SWAT team five minutes down the road on permanent standby. As soon as you know what the plan is I want you to hit that button on your watch and we'll come in for you. You tell us what's happening and we'll take over."

"Understood."

Wallace placed his hand on Jack's shoulder. "I mean it," he said.

"I understand. And thank you for what you said about... you know."

"No son, thank you. This is a good thing you're doing."

Wallace pulled his helmet back on and without another word he kicked out the door wedge and left.

CHAPTER SIXTEEN

Jack didn't get chance to pursue his new goal before dinner that night. Jack and Abi had left the GamesCon about an hour later. Jack wanted to come up with some ideas for how to find out what was going on so he claimed he was tired after the morning's events and wanted to go to his room to rest. Abi didn't press him. Before he had the time to get any real thinking done, though, Sandra came round to collect the beta testers and take them to the canteen beside the GameZone.

The testers split up into their usual little groups but the conversation in most of them seemed to be about the same thing. The Elites who'd been on stage that afternoon.

They were still being kept separate from the rest of the testers but every discussion seemed to be about them, including Jack and Abi's. Although he suspected that the reason for his interest was very different to the others.

"How were they picked?" Jack asked Abi. He hadn't told Abi that he'd recognised them from the night before and she hadn't said anything herself so he figured she hadn't realised.

"They were the top players in the first week based on their skill in all of the games."

The lad on her other side overheard and joined in.

"It wasn't just that though. I never really understood how they picked them because I was definitely better than some of them."

Abi turned so that only Jack could see her face and winked at him. Then she turned back to the other tester and spoke slowly as though to a particularly stupid infant.

"Sandra and Alex explained it to us in the beginning, remember? It was based on performance over a variety of games, and they used weighted averages and things. They said it wouldn't be obvious." The lad shrugged and turned away, losing interest in the discussion now that they hadn't simply agreed with him.

"Why do you ask?" Abi asked Jack.

"Just wondered. They looked so cool I wanted to know what I'd have to do to join them."

"Oh, I think you're too late now," Abi said. "Anyway, if you were part of their group you wouldn't get to play with me. I don't imagine it's worth giving that up for a silver spacesuit!"

Jack laughed and they ate without speaking for a while, comfortable in each other's company without needing to talk. Jack was glad he'd found someone he could rely on here.

As he ate he became aware of a group in the corner laughing louder than normal. Jack raised his head past Abi to see who it was. It was Sebastien and his stupid mates. They caught Jack's eye and burst out laughing again.

Idiots, he thought and quickly dismissed them from his mind when he saw Veteran drop his empty dinner tray off and walk towards him on his way to the door.

Yes, he's coming this way! Despite playing with the guy for days now he still hadn't lost his fanboy status as far as Veteran was concerned. If he could think of a casual way to ask for his autograph before they went he would definitely do it.

Veteran stopped at their table and leant on the back of Jack's chair.

"You okay after earlier Jack?" he asked.

"Yeah, I'm alright now."

"That was crap that was, you should complain about it to Sauer. You never know, they might give you some extra freebies!" his eyes twinkled.

"Yeah, maybe I will," Jack said, at the same time thinking, *No, I won't!*

"Anyway, just ignore those guys." Veteran flicked his head towards Sebastien's little group. "They're prats."

"Thanks."

"I'm going to turn in. See you tomorrow."

"Yeah, see you tomorrow." Veteran sauntered off and Jack turned back to Abi. "What does he mean 'ignore them'?"

"I don't know."

More people had joined the group in the corner and they laughed again. This time there was no mistaking it, right after the laughter a good third of the group turned and looked over in his direction.

Jack pushed his seat back and stood. "I'm going to find out what's going on over there."

"Just ignore them Jack. Veteran is right, whatever they're doing they're just idiots."

But Jack had already started to walk away. She rolled her eyes and followed him.

He joined the back of the group and pushed his way through.

"Excuse me," he said moving people out of the way. To his surprise they all parted and made a path for him.

Sebastien was sitting at the table at the centre of the group. His tablet was on the screen in front of him playing a video on a loop.

He nodded at Jack and for a split second Jack half thought he was about to apologise. He shouldn't have been so stupid.

"Here he is," Sebastien said, his accent thicker than usual. "The, how do you say? Man... no... boy, of the hour!"

Most of the group laughed and Jack felt his face going red. He didn't know what all of this was about but he regretted coming over now. Behind him Abi had caught up with him and she obviously felt the same way.

"Come on Jack, let's get out of here," she said.

"Non, non. Surely Jackie wants to see his moment of glory? Here let me help everyone get a better view."

He climbed up on his chair and held up the tablet towards Jack.

On the screen Jack saw himself lying on the floor of the GameZone shaking. Somehow Sebastien had taken a video grab of the scene from his glasses when he was shooting Jack and changed it so that it showed Jack as himself, not looking like the terrorist in the way that the GamesCon audience had seen.

"Theess is my favourite beet coming now," Sebastien said and raised the volume just in time. The tablet's little speakers played Jack's voice begging.

It was mortifying but Jack knew that worse was coming. Sure enough a couple of seconds later, when the volley of shots from all three of the hunters had hit him, Jack saw himself lose consciousness.

"Look, look, 'ee faints!" Sebastien said through his laughter. Genuine tears were rolling down his face. Jack didn't know what he'd done to this boy other than not know who his stupid mother was but he was obviously using Jack to work out some real issues.

He thanked God again that he hadn't lost control of his bladder. The embarrassment would have been unbearable.

"I didn't faint. I blacked out," Jack heard himself saying. Even he thought it was weak.

Sebastien was about to reply but Abi got in first.

"That's enough Sebastien," she said forcefully.

"Mais non! I am afraid it is not enough. My mother will be here tomorrow with all of the news cameras that follow her around. I am going to spend as much time as I can with her and whenever I can I am going to have this weeth me playing. Watch the news tomorrow Jackie and if we are lucky you will be on it. You will be famous!"

Jack didn't know what to do. He wanted to kill Sebastien there and then. He was a spy for God's sake. He was trying to do something good. He thought of the bag of tricks that Alice had given him and whether he could use any of it on Sebastien, perhaps throw one of the smoke grenades into his bedroom and choke him, or strangle him with his hi-tension bracelet cord. But he knew he couldn't.

He settled for turning and walking away.

"Au revoir Jackie. Sleep well!" Sebastien called from behind him.

For the second time that night Abi ran after him. She caught up to him just as he reached the door.

Sandra was already standing there, looking very sorry.

"I'm sorry Jack, I don't have the power to take it off him. If I did, I would," she said.

"I'd like to go back to my room please," Jack said simply.

Sandra exchanged a look with Abi.

"I'll take him," Abi said and Sandra opened the door.

In the corridor Abi took him by both shoulders.

"He doesn't matter Jack. You know that, right? He's a nobody, trading on his mother's name."

Jack nodded.

"Thanks Abi, but right now I don't want to talk. I just want to go to bed."

She led him upstairs silently, afraid to leave him alone. When they reached his door she spoke again.

"Will you be alright? You could sleep in my room. I could use the settee."

Jack smiled weakly at her, "I'm okay, really. I just want to have some time alone. Do you mind?"

She smiled back and watched him into his room.

When the door was shut he sagged down onto the edge of his bed and kicked off his shoes.

He knew she was right. Sebastien didn't matter. Hell, Sebastien didn't even know his real surname. And Jack should be concentrating on finding out what Morton, or Sauer, was planning.

But nobody needed this sort of thing.

He lay back on the bed.

He should check the message board and see if Wallace had found anything out. And if not then he needed to think about how he could do it himself.

Maybe I could use Sandra? Sauer always seems to be unkind to her, perhaps she knows something.

He closed his eyes to think and, before he could stop himself, he was asleep.

CHAPTER SEVENTEEN

Jack woke with a start.

Oh God, what time is it? he thought.

His mouth was dry and his neck ached from where he had slept awkwardly, lying on the edge of the bed with his feet on the floor. He struggled up and checked the time on the little clock on the bedside cabinet.

07:15

Damn. I slept all through the night. I was supposed to go out again last night and see if I could find out what's going on.

He felt like someone had hit him with a bat while he slept. He forced himself to stand up and blundered into the bathroom to splash water on his face so he would wake up properly.

He started to brush his teeth while he grabbed his phone and checked the SWAT Team IV bulletin board for any messages from Wallace.

He scrolled through only half paying attention. He wasn't really expecting them to come back with anything useful. Wallace had pretty much said it was down to him to find out what was going on, but to his surprise there was a message.

At 02:11 a user called WallBoy had posted what looked like the results of a game he had been in. Jack knew otherwise. It was a message from Wallace. He went and got his book and sat on the edge of his bed to begin the laborious job of decoding it.

The losing team's score in each round was the page number and the number of shots fired was the number of the word on the page. It was slow going but Alice's staff at CIRCLE had explained to him that it was worth it. Unless you knew which book to use it was technically unbreakable.

Half way through he forgot about brushing his teeth and shook his head slowly, his toothbrush hanging out of his mouth stupidly. He couldn't believe what he was decoding.

He tried to speed up until eventually he had the whole message spelt out in front of him.

> Abi is not to be trusted. Her surname is Morton. She is Simon's daughter. Stay away from her.

He stared at the message until it became a jumble of meaningless letters. It didn't make sense.

They must be wrong. He pulled a face, thinking of all of the people he'd seen at CIRCLE headquarters and, as much as he wanted to, he couldn't bring himself to believe that. They wouldn't have got something like this wrong. Then it struck him, if it was true he could verify it for himself easily enough. A man like Morton was always in the public eye.

He grabbed up his phone and did a search for Abi Morton. He flicked over to the images page and sure enough, there she was. The first result was a picture from when she was younger, she was at some sort of celebrity event, presumably one of Morton's launches, and she was standing between her mother and father.

His shoulders slumped. *They were right. I mean, of course they were right but still...*

It was definitely her. He couldn't believe how gullible he had been. A single internet search was all it had taken. Why hadn't he done that before?

A proper spy would have checked. But why would I? She didn't give me any reason to think she was anything other than she seemed.

And maybe she wasn't. She was obviously his daughter but so what? That didn't mean she had to be involved. She couldn't be. She was his friend.

A friend he had only known for a couple of days.

And I didn't even know her surname.

And if she wasn't involved then why hadn't she told him who her dad was? She must have something to hide.

Then he remembered, she had almost told him, "I'm just someone's daughter, like Sebastien." she'd said.

This is no good, he thought and stood up. *I have to talk to her. I have to understand what is going on.*

Jack practically ran to Abi's bedroom and this time he didn't knock quietly at all. He banged on her door and stood there angrily.

And then, while he waited for her to answer, his mind went blank. What was he supposed to say?

He had stormed round here determined to have it out with her but now he wasn't so sure. How did he start that conversation? What was he accusing her of anyway? Surely not really being involved in a plan to control people's minds? She was a child for God's sake!

I'm a child though and I'm involved.

But it was different for her. If she was involved then she'd be on the wrong side. And that didn't fit with what he knew about her.

All of that and more tumbled through his head as she walked to the door. But it didn't tumble fast enough to finish before she answered and noticed something was wrong.

"What's up Jack?" she asked looking concerned. "Are you still upset about Sebastien?"

"I... no... can I come in for a minute?"

"Of course. I was just going to get ready to call one of the staff to escort me down for breakfast but it can wait. Come in."

Jack went in and sat on the chair in the corner. Abi sat on her bed and drew her feet up to sit cross legged.

"So what is it? You look like you've got something to say."

Jack hesitated and then leapt at it. He was pretty sure this wasn't how a spy would handle it but then if CIRCLE wanted him to act like a spy then they'd need to teach him. For now all he could do was act like himself.

"You didn't tell me who your dad was," he said simply. As he spoke he decided not to attack her, he hoped she'd have an explanation and he wanted to give her chance to give it to him.

She nodded slowly and uncurled her legs so that she was sitting on the edge of the bed.

"No, I didn't. But now you know. How?"

Jack actually had prepared an answer for that.

"Veteran told me." She nodded. It was a bluff but it had worked. He'd hoped that at least one of the other testers would know and if one of them did it would be possible they'd talked. She didn't make anything of it so it must have worked.

"Does it matter?" she asked.

"Does it matter?!" he repeated in disbelief. His plan not to attack her falling at the first hurdle. "Of course it matters. I was sneaking around trying to find things out, telling you something terrible was going on at Morton Tech." Her eyes narrowed as he said that but he didn't notice. "And all the while it was your dad."

"That doesn't mean I agree with everything that's going on here. Or even that I know what is."

He hesitated, the passion draining from him, "No," he said. "I suppose not. But you should have told me."

Abi appeared to deflate, all of the strength went out of her and she looked like a little girl.

"I'm sorry Jack. I thought perhaps if it came to it then it would be useful later, you know if you found anything to write a story about."

Ah yes, my trainee journalist cover, he thought guiltily.

He looked at her now. He'd stormed in here, cross with her for lying to him and she obviously felt bad about it, but he'd been lying to her as well and it hadn't even occurred to him. Now *he* felt bad.

However this ended it wasn't going to go well for her. If CIRCLE managed to stop Shark then she was going to lose her dad and if they didn't... if whatever he'd got planned worked... Well, that couldn't be good for her either. He didn't think the world would be kind to the children of criminal geniuses. All of his anger left him and he was just worried for her.

He glanced at his watch. He didn't have long, he had to get on with finding out what Morton had planned and work out a way to stop him, but he had to do something for Abi first. He didn't know how much to tell her but looking at her now he wanted to help her.

Maybe if she put some distance between herself and Morton Tech before it all broke, he thought.

He went and sat down on the bed next to her.

"You've never mentioned your mother to me. Well, you never mentioned your dad either..." he rolled this eyes and started to get annoyed again but she rested a hand on his leg and he calmed down. *Got to stay on topic,* he thought. "Where is she? Perhaps you could spend some time with her."

Abi looked away for a minute and then spoke without meeting his eyes.

"She's in an institution."

"An institution?" Jack parroted stupidly.

"A mental institution, Jack," Abi said pronouncing every word carefully. "For insane people."

"Oh... oh... I'm sorry. So you can't go and live with her?"

"No Jack."

"Of course. Of course." None of this was going as he'd planned. "I'm sorry I asked. I just thought if you had to leave here, then you'd need..."

"Why would I leave here?" she interrupted, looking directly at him again.

He took a deep breath and plunged in.

"I wasn't trying to find a news story Abi. There is something going on here. Something that is very bad and I don't think it's going to go well for your dad or Sauer or anyone who's involved. I want you to get away from him."

"What is it? Do you know?"

"It's Shark, it's a mind control device."

"No!" Abi said. "Who knows that?"

"Just me and an organisation I'm working for."

"What organisation?" Her eyes narrowed.

"It's a long story."

"Well can't this organisation stop it, whoever they are?"

"They don't know what's going to happen. I need to find out and then stop it if I can."

"Why you?" Abi asked, confused.

"It's difficult to explain. There's a lot you don't know about me."

She stood up and started pacing in front of him. After a moment she came to a decision.

"I'll help you," she said.

"No, it's too dangerous."

"He's still my dad. If he's involved, then he'll listen to me. And besides, yesterday you said you thought Sauer was in charge. Maybe you were right, maybe it's not my dad at all. In that case he'll help us."

Jack hesitated, he didn't know what to think. Yesterday he had felt terrible for getting her involved at all, then this morning he'd come here thinking she was hiding things from him and determined to have it out with her, and now she was throwing herself even deeper in.

She sensed his indecision and insisted.

"I can help Jack."

She had stopped pacing and was standing directly in front of him.

"If I said yes, then what do you think we should do?"

"I think we should go and confront my dad. You said you don't know what's happening, but he will. Whether it's him or Sauer he'll know what's going on or he'll know what to do. I say we go now, together, and see what he has to say."

"Where will he be?" Jack asked, coming around to her idea. It was nice to have someone on his side for a change.

"In his suite of course. Where he always is. Come on."

CHAPTER EIGHTEEN

They had already left Abi's room and were hurrying down the corridor to the central reception area so they could get the lift to Morton's suite, when Abi asked a question that floored Jack.

"Can you get us in?"

Jack stopped dead in his tracks.

"To your dad's suite? Can't you?" he asked

"They'll let me in if I ask but then they'll know we're coming. I thought it would be better it if it was a surprise."

That was a good point. He didn't have much of a plan but if he was going to confront an adult billionaire then he reckoned that surprise would be an advantage. And he could use all the advantages he could get.

"Yes, a surprise would definitely be better," he said.

"I assume this organisation of yours is who gave you your special spy tools. The amazing gloves and bugs."

"Yes. They did."

"Not an online shop from Omaha then."

"Ah." Another lie he'd told her. "No. Not an online shop."

"I figured. Anyway, didn't they give you anything that could get us in without them knowing we were coming?"

"Oh wait yes! Is Sauer allowed into your dad's suite?"

"Yes, he can come and go as he pleases."

"Then I have just the thing," Jack said and produced his phone from his pocket. He opened the card reading app Alice had put on it for him and swiped through it until he came to the copy he had taken of Sauer's ID. "This is supposed to take a copy of any magnetic card. Credit cards, debit cards..."

"ID cards!" Abi said.

"Exactly."

"But how did you get Sauer's?" There was a note of admiration in Abi's voice that Jack appreciated.

"On the first day when I went to the toilet and he brought me back to the GameZone. I bumped into him 'by accident' and took a copy then."

"That's brilliant."

"Maybe, but to be honest I don't know if it really works. I haven't had to use them at all. We'll need to check before we try using it there."

"The GameZone is access controlled, we could use that. It's on the way to reception anyway."

"Okay."

They arrived at the GameZone three minutes later. Jack held his phone against the reader and the light turned green. He grinned and tried the door just to prove it to himself.

Abi was a couple of steps behind him so she heard him groan a second before she saw the reason.

"Hello Jackie!"

"Hello Sebastien," Jack said with a sigh.

Sebastien blocked the doorway and peered past Jack over the top of his Shark glasses. He was obviously expecting to see one of the staff and Jack realised straight away that the little snake was trying to decide how unkind to be depending on who was with them. Of course there was no member of staff at all and the French boy was instantly suspicious.

"Who let you in?" he demanded. "What's that in your hand? You're not supposed to have an access card you know."

"I don't have time for this Sebastien," Jack said.

"No, well that's a shame. I'll just go and get Sandra and see what she thinks about it. It might be too late to be kicked off the beta testing team but I'm sure they wouldn't want to give the free samples to people who'd been breaking the rules."

Abi stepped in front of Jack.

"Go and call the lift Jack, I'll handle this," she said.

Jack stared at her without understanding. Her right hand went to her pocket but she pulled the GameZone door shut behind her with her left, shutting off Jack's view.

He smiled, he didn't know what she was going to do but he assumed she was about to pull rank on Sebastien. There must be some benefits to being Morton's daughter after all. He crossed reception and pressed the button to call the lift, unable to keep a big grin off his face.

She was back at his side before the lift had even had time to arrive.

"That was quick. What did you say to him? Or did you tell Sandra about him?" Jack asked, the delight obvious in his voice.

"I just explained we'd got something important to do and he should grow up."

She obviously didn't want to tell him and for now there were more important things to take care of but he decided he'd have to get it out of her later.

The lift doors opened with a 'ping' noise and Abi stepped inside without another word. Jack followed her and waited for the doors to close behind them. Luckily nobody else got in at the same time.

"Are you sure you want to do this?" he asked, his hand hovering over the bank of buttons.

"Absolutely. Press the button."

He pressed the one for the top floor suite and the lift began its rapid, stomach churning hurtle upwards through the building.

"When we're in there, leave it to me at first," Jack said. "If he doesn't cooperate then you can do the daughter thing."

"How very chivalrous of you," Abi said with a hint of a smile.

He did want to protect Abi but if he was honest with himself he also wanted to do everything he could to make sure that CIRCLE knew it was him who had stopped Morton. Then they'd have to get Bobby out of trouble.

The lift doors opened with the same 'ping' as downstairs, but now that they were trying to be discreet it sounded incredibly loud to Jack. The doors started to open and he suddenly remembered Morton's receptionist sat right in front of them.

"What about his secretary?" he whispered to Abi.

"She doesn't start until eight o'clock. We'll be fine."

Sure enough the doors opened and the desk was empty. *Thank God,* he thought.

"What about your dad, will he be here? When does he start work?"

"He'll be here. This is where he sleeps now."

There was a bitterness in her voice that Jack hadn't heard before but he put it down to the stress of confronting her father.

"Come on then, let's do this," he said, taking charge again.

He led the way across the big reception area and held his phone against the reader.

The light turned green and he breathed out, realising at the same time that he'd been holding his breath.

"Ready?" he asked her.

Abi nodded once.

Jack opened the door and in the same move swept dramatically into Morton's palatial suite.

Morton might sleep in the room but he wasn't sleeping now. He was sitting behind the big desk with his back to the fantastic view Jack had admired when he was last in here.

"Jack Dawson," he said calmly when Jack burst through the door. "And my Abi, how lovely."

Jack crossed the room as quickly as he could and stood before the man who owned the building and who he assumed was behind the terrible scheme he'd uncovered.

In the corner of his eye he saw Abi peel off from him and head to the other side of the room out of sight, but he stuck to the plan and launched straight into Morton.

"We know what's going on, Morton!" he said. Morton raised an eyebrow and Jack instantly corrected himself. "Mr Morton."

"What's that then, lad?" Morton said seeming amused rather than outraged by this interruption.

"Shark. We know that it's some way of controlling people's minds. We know that you have something planned for it. We know about the people who died and that the Elites are totally under your control."

Morton's smile became tense halfway through Jack's little speech. By the time Jack had finished he looked positively wooden.

Jack waited for him to respond but there was nothing. He didn't even move.

"Mr Morton. Simon!" Jack prompted.

Morton came back to the room with a blink but instead of replying to Jack he looked past him. Jack looked over his shoulder and saw that he was looking towards Abi. She was hunched over a computer in the corner.

"Abi," Morton said. "What do I do, my love?"

Jack's mouth dropped open and he turned to look fully at Abi.

He looked back to Morton, looking for any sign of a trick or a distraction but there was nothing there. The man seemed genuinely to be waiting on instructions from his teenage daughter. He looked back to Abi.

"Oh God!" Jack said as it dawned on him.

"I'm afraid so," Abi said, straightening up from the computer.

Jack's brain reeled trying to make sense of what he was seeing. It was still Abi, it still sounded like her and looked like her but at the same time she had become an entirely different person. Something in the way she held herself had changed. She seemed slightly taller and there was an edge to her voice that hadn't been there before.

"I'll stop you," he said to her.

"Stop me doing what Jack? You still don't know, so don't embarrass yourself." She sounded matter of fact but certainly not unkind.

Jack was still struggling to process any of it as the door to the suite opened again and three members of the Elites walked in. They had their Shark glasses on and their faces had that sickly pallor from the blue light that spilled from them.

"You," Abi said and pointed at one of them, a tall, well built twenty-something man that Jack didn't recognise. "Take anything electronic he has on him. Oh, and his shoes."

The man started walking towards him with a vacant expression and Abi spoke again, this time to Jack. "I'd hand them over if I were you, Jack. He's bigger than you and the mind control isn't very sophisticated. It doesn't really give them much room to be gentle."

Jack shrugged and took his phone from his pocket.

The man had reached him and Jack stretched his arm out to hand him the phone, his sleeve slid up his arm slightly and the man's hand flashed out as quick as lightning and grabbed Jack's wrist.

"Your watch," he said in a flat voice.

Damn! The watch was electronic so he was going to take it. Jack briefly wondered if he had time to press the panic sequence and call in CIRCLE but the man was already tugging at it.

He undid the strap before the Player damaged his wrist.

Abi tilted her head slightly and glanced down at his shoes. "Quickly Jack, they don't react well if there's a delay in carrying out their instructions."

Jack pushed his shoes with the gecko soles off and kicked them over, though what Abi thought he'd do with them he had no idea. He definitely wasn't going to make a break for it and walk down the outside of the building. Even if he was brave enough at this height he'd be blown off by the wind.

"Empty your pockets," the man said.

Jack threw his keys and wallet onto Morton's desk and pulled his pockets inside out so that they could see they were empty.

The man turned back to Abi.

"Done."

"Okay, go and stand by the door. No one leaves here until I say."

He nodded and strode back to the doorway where he stood right in the middle like a solider at attention, legs slightly apart and arms ramrod straight at either side, one hand still holding Jack's phone and watch since Abi hadn't given him an instruction to put them down.

He almost filled the doorway and Jack didn't fancy his chances of getting past him.

Now that Abi was satisfied that Jack wasn't a threat she strolled casually to the long table in front of the video conferencing screen as though she owned the whole place. She pulled a mini tablet like Sandra's from her pocket, threw it carelessly onto the table so that she could sit more easily, and dropped into one of the seats.

The table had been set for dinner when Jack was here before, but without the tablecloth, candlesticks and cutlery it was clearly a meeting room table. It looked every bit as impressive as the boardroom table downstairs and Jack had to admit she fitted comfortably behind it.

The other two Elites, who were both girls in their late teens followed her and stood behind her, one on either side, the same faraway look on their faces as Simon Morton and the doorman had.

Now what do I do? Jack thought. *Is this it, is it all over because I didn't see it was her? No!* he decided, *I'm not giving up. I don't care if it's Morton or her, it doesn't make any difference. I still have to stop her. But stop her doing what?*

She was right, he still didn't know what her plan really was. He needed to understand what was going on if he stood any chance of stopping it.

She didn't seem to be in any hurry to leave, so Jack spoke as casually as he could to try to weasel her plan out of her.

"If it was you all along then why pretend to help me at all?"

"I needed to know if you were working alone. Shark was well in hand and I had some spare time. And honestly? It was fun watching you blunder about trying to work it out. Haven't you ever watched the stupid kids mess stuff up? That's what it's like for me with you."

He shook his head. She was right of course. She was much smarter than him.

"Was anything you told me true?"

"My name. And the fact that stupid people irritate me."

"You didn't tell me the most important part of your name," Jack said, a flash of the bitterness he felt showing in his voice.

"Oh, true. Just the bit about the stupid people then."

She said it with a smile as though the whole thing were a game to her, which he supposed it was. He was about to ask why she was doing all of this when he was interrupted by her phone buzzing. She looked down at it and read the message she had received.

"Ah, here we go," she said to her father. "The president's plane has landed. You need to go and meet her. You know what to do?"

"Yes," Morton replied in a monotone, rising from behind the desk as he spoke. When he was fully stood up his glasses flashed and his face changed, the muscles tightened slightly in a way that Jack had come to recognise as the face of someone with an implanted programme. "Abi!" he said, as though waking up. "I've got to go and meet Madame President now, will you be alright here with your friends for a while?"

"Of course Dad," she said lightly, her voice just like the one Jack remembered from before. "I'll see you after the launch. Good luck!"

"Thanks my love," he said and walked to the door, every bit the successful billionaire Jack had been expecting to meet before all of this began.

Abi watched him over her shoulder and then spoke quietly to the older of the two girls, "Go with him to security and make sure he gets there okay."

The girl fell in behind Morton and the two of them left the room, the doorman standing aside at a nod from Abi.

When they had gone Abi brought her attention back to Jack and Jack tried again to get her to tell him what she had planned.

"So you keep your dad locked up in here?"

"He's not locked up. I just implanted the idea that he wanted to stay in here in his head a couple of months ago when he started asking awkward questions. You need to be really careful with adults, Jack, their brains are brittle."

"Brittle?"

"They snap too easily. At first all of my subjects were adults but the conditioning has to bend the mind that it's working on and adults... well most of them tend to break not bend."

"The suicides."

"Exactly! That was unfortunate, we had to learn to be more subtle. You see, you can implant an instruction gradually over time so you don't need to control them in the moment, or you can just override the mind through the senses like we do in the game," she waved at the tablet on the table. "Adults in particular can react badly to the override. Brittle, like I said. Some of them are okay but the more you use them the more likely they are to snap. Especially if you're getting them to do something they wouldn't want to themselves. Only a very tiny percentage of them last longer than a month. Most break almost immediately. I nearly gave up, but luckily we learnt that children's minds are so much more flexible. We're perfect for this really, Jack. Soon I could have everyone under the age of about twenty as my own private puppet show."

"What about Sauer, is he in on it?"

"Depends what you mean by 'in on it'. He's one of the very few adults who took the conditioning well. Though if I'm honest I think that might be because he secretly wanted this sort of thing anyway. You were right about him being an unpleasant man. He was that before I had anything to do with him. Anyway, whatever the reason, the conditioning works on him and he does what I tell him."

"That's why he didn't see us that night in the Elites' room."

"No, actually that was your quick thinking and wall climbing things. Very impressive. But it wouldn't have mattered if he had seen us. At least to me. I could have dealt with him."

Jack still couldn't bring himself to believe it was her.

"But why, why do it at all?"

Abi laughed, genuinely entertained. He remembered them both laughing in the restaurant and it was still the very same carefree laugh but he couldn't match the sound to the terrible things she was talking about.

"All these questions, Jack. Still trying to work it out! But the real question is, why not? Money. Power. Boredom. Take your pick. Mainly boredom. *You* know what it's like having to slow down for everyone around you. Come on!" She waved her arms in exasperation. "But really, just think about it, an army of people under my control. They could do anything, people would pay us a fortune for them. But first I need a demonstration."

Jack frowned, the pieces were starting to fit into an ugly picture in his head. He still had to ask though.

"A demonstration?"

"Yes, you'll like this. I'm going to have Sebastien kill his mother on international television. What better demonstration could there be than someone killing their parent. And such a mummy's boy as well! There'll be no doubting the power of Shark when that's happened."

"But for it to work as a demonstration everyone would have to know it wasn't him. You'll be arrested."

"No, only the right people need to know it wasn't him. To the rest of the world he'll just be one more crazy lone killer. You should be pleased, Jack. An hour from now Sebastien will either be killed by French security or be under arrest. Or maybe I'll have him kill himself. Yes, that will be neater."

Jack was flabbergasted. Even with everything else she had admitted he had never thought she would plan a murder. And to use Sebastien against his own mother. It was diabolical but if he put himself in her position it made a twisted sort of sense.

"So that's why you went through the charade of getting me to break in here this morning. The timing of the president's visit. I assume you do have a key really."

"Of course I do. But you got to me slightly earlier than I was expecting, well done for that by the way, so I needed to delay you. I couldn't have you running around bumping into her security detail and frightening them."

Jack nodded and then a thought occurred to him.

That's how she stopped Sebastien this morning, she had already got him under control ready.

"How long have you been controlling him? Has he been behaving like that to me since I got here because of you?"

"No!" Abi said with the most emotion he'd seen from her since they got up here. "No, I wouldn't do that to you. He's just an idiot like I told you from day one. His Shark conditioning won't have any impact on him until I'm ready."

For some reason Jack was pleased about that.

"So what now then? Is this where you ask me to join you or are you going to kill me?"

"Oh I don't believe for a minute that you'd join me!"

Jack hid his disappointment, tricking her into thinking he was on her side had been his last idea. But her face matched her words, there was no way she would buy it.

"There's no point carrying on," he said. "CIRCLE knows about Shark. If Sebastien kills his mum then even if the rest of the world believes he was acting on his own they'll know and they'll come for you."

"Oh come on, Jack, no-one's going to suspect me are they? I'm a little girl." She batted her eyelashes at him and for a second her face lost all of its hard edges and she was the girl he'd known before. "Yes, thanks to you they'll work out that he was under someone's control, but that will be my dad's last present for me. They'll think it was him and I'll be long gone before anyone suspects me."

Jack was silent for a minute but there was really very little left to say. He couldn't talk her out of it and he couldn't stop it from here. He'd lost. Sebastien's mother was going to die and more importantly to him, even though he knew it was selfish, Bobby would go to jail.

"So what about me then, what are you going to do with me?"

She frowned.

"I don't know. I'll deal with you when I come back. I don't want to kill you but if I can't think of any alternative while I'm downstairs then I guess I will have to." She laughed again, the same sweet laugh despite the fact that she was talking about killing him. "Well, *I* won't obviously. I'll make someone else do it!"

Then she jumped up from the table and skipped happily from the room, the other girl following vacantly behind.

CHAPTER NINETEEN

At first Jack didn't react quite as heroically as he would have liked.

His initial reaction was to wallow in self pity. Only when he thought about how his inevitable death would mean that Bobby would never get out did he stop wallowing. And even then it was only because an imaginary version of Bobby gave him a kick up the arse.

Hawkes don't give up, man, he heard Bobby's voice in his head tell him.

Jack looked at the stocky man blocking the door. There was no way he was getting past him.

No? When was the last time a Hawke was trapped in a room by an evil teenage girl-genius who was trying to take over the world?

That's a girl?! Imaginary-Bobby said, looking through Jack's eyes.

No, that's her brainless bodybuilding guard.

You can out-smart a zombie, Jack.

And then what, what do I do when I'm out?

Actually the answer to that was simple. He knew what was happening now and he knew where it was going to

165

happen. Abi wanted to do it in front of all of the cameras so that meant she'd do it at the launch. All he had to do was get out of here, get to the launch, into the VIP area, past the president's security, the English police and the mind controlled Elites Abi would probably have set up as guards, and then save the president of France from her unintentionally murderous (but intentionally irritating) son.

Imaginary-Bobby rolled his imaginary eyes. *Jeez, I don't know what the big deal is. Why are you sitting here talking to me? Get on with it.*

Jack grinned and the ridiculousness of the situation struck him.

Oh well, one problem at a time. First he had to get out of here or the rest of it wouldn't matter anyway.

He looked at the clock on Morton's desk. 10:06. Assuming she timed it for the moment of the official launch he had twenty four minutes.

He stood up and walked around the room, sizing up his opportunities. The doorman did nothing. Presumably he didn't have enough self control left to notice that Jack's behaviour had changed.

Abi had made sure that Jack didn't have his most exciting toys but she didn't know about all of them and she'd assumed anything else he had would be electronic. He briefly considered garrotting the doorman but his mind put paid to that idea very quickly. The doorman would demolish him in any hand to hand struggle, brain or no brain. His imagination delivered its verdict by way of a mental image of the doorman sitting on top of him, Jack securely tied up like a Christmas present with his own high tensile cord.

He ruled that out.

He kept pacing around the huge penthouse. Maybe he could use the video conference and get a message to CIRCLE. But what then? They wouldn't have time to get here and do anything. Besides, he didn't have a phone number for them and he doubted their headquarters would be listed in directory enquiries.

Scratch that plan too.

Jack's wandering had brought him to the glass wall that ran a third of the way down Morton's suite and he bent to examine it, wondering if he would be able to break through it and get out that way. He glanced over at the doorman, he was still ignoring him. The glass was a non-starter though, it was triple-glazed. There was no way Jack was strong enough to break it.

He carried on around the room and saw that Abi had left her tablet on the long table. He guessed whatever she had done to Sebastien was sufficiently embedded that she didn't need it any more, but it might come in handy for him. He picked it up in full view of the doorman to test his reaction. If he objected then Jack would just put it down fast. He didn't seem to care. Obviously Abi's instructions didn't extend to making sure he didn't steal things. He slipped the tablet into his pocket and kept walking.

He paused behind Morton's desk and looked out at his magnificent view again. He didn't envy the man this time, though. Jack would rather do without the penthouse suite and amazing view if it meant not having a murderous genius daughter.

His eye fell on the handle to the window and he wondered. He lay his hand on the handle and lifted slightly. The window opened a crack and he leant forward enough to see the vertiginous drop. Then he heard a noise directly behind him. He turned and nearly jumped out of his skin. The doorman was standing two feet behind him looming over him.

"You are not to leave."

Jack raised his hands in a conciliatory gesture.

"I know, I know, easy big boy. I'm just getting some air."

He eyed the door some way behind the doorman.

Could I beat him back over there? he thought. His imagination delivered its verdict in a very similar mental image to his earlier garrotting idea. The only difference was that this time he wasn't actually tied up. There was no way he'd get the door open and get out before the doorman caught him.

His problem was that the penthouse might be massive for a room but it was all open plan and it wasn't big enough for him to do anything without the doorman seeing him and triggering his conditioning.

While Jack thought the doorman ambled back over to the door and turned back into a flesh statue.

But he has to see me do something that breaks his instructions, right? Otherwise he just stands there and waits. He did nothing while I fiddled with the video conference, it was only when he saw me open the window that he reacted.

His wallet and his key ring were sitting on Morton's desk. His wallet was his own but the keys were the ones Alice had given him. The smoke grenades.

If the doorman didn't see him then he wouldn't react.

And if the room was full of smoke he wouldn't be able to see him.

He wondered if the doorman would have enough self preservation left to react to the smoke or if he would simply stay still. Either way, it would give Jack a chance.

But a chance to do what? He still couldn't get past him. The man was physically blocking the door.

Jack bent and picked his keys and wallet up as calmly as he could, watching the doorman out of the corner of his eye. He didn't react.

He felt the wind on his face as he ducked past the level of the window and a plan started to form in his head. He didn't like it at all. His imagination did its helpful trick of offering up a possible ending but this one didn't involve the doorman sitting on him.

It was the only idea he had.

All he had to do was trust Alice.

He took his bracelet from his wrist and started unwinding it, half hoping the doorman would come and stop him.

Jack prepared for his escape plan as quickly as he could.

He looped one end of the super strong bracelet cord around a leg of the heavy desk and tried pulling with all his strength. It didn't budge and he was confident it would take his weight.

He was as discreet as he could be but he was pretty certain the doorman must have seen some of it. As far as Jack could tell through the Shark glasses, he had been staring in his direction the whole time but he didn't appear to have any understanding of what Jack was doing. At least he didn't make a move to stop him.

He thought about trying to get his gloves and shoes from the little table that the doorman had put them on but it was too risky. Anyway, people abseiled all the time and none of them had special gecko shoes.

He strolled over to the other side of the room, shoving his hands into his pocket and taking hold of his bunch of keys tightly. The doorman's head tracked him as he moved but, as he wasn't heading for the window and there was no way he'd get through the door, he didn't move.

Alice had suggested that he use one key at a time, but he didn't have the chance to take one off the ring so he would just have to use them all. Annoyingly because they were a catalyst not the generator themselves it wouldn't mean there was any more smoke.

It might mean it's a bit faster, he thought, pleasantly surprised to have a fact from school chemistry pop into his head and be useful for a change.

Jack reached the nice big tropical fish tank and stood still for a minute. He'd noticed that whenever he stopped moving the doorman stopped looking at him. Sure enough a minute later the big man's head drifted round until he was staring forward blankly again.

Sorry guys, Jack thought to the fish and dropped the keys into the tank. They settled slowly through the water. *I wonder how long it will...*

Before he could finish the thought the fish tank erupted in a billowing cloud of water vapour. Alice was right, it was so dense it might as well have been smoke. He stood very still and waited for the cloud to surround him, the doorman didn't move. When the smoke was too thick for him to see the doorman he ducked down behind the table and listened. Nothing. It had worked. The doorman couldn't see him so he wasn't reacting.

Staying low to the floor, he crawled as quickly and quietly as he could back to the desk. He yanked off his socks and stuck them over his hands to give them some protection then grabbed up the ends of the cord and stepped to the window.

He swallowed nervously then climbed carefully up onto the ledge and risked a look back over to the doorman.

The fish tank was still bubbling, smoke pouring out of the top of it. The only movement in the smoke was from the tank itself, so he figured it had worked. The doorman couldn't see or hear anything and he didn't have enough initiative of his own left to investigate, so he hadn't moved at all.

There couldn't be much water left in the tank so Jack leant backwards over the edge of the window clasping the cord tightly in both sock-covered hands.

He froze. It was terrifying and completely unnatural to lower yourself backwards over a drop like this.

He stood there for what felt like forever clutching the loop of cord in his hands like the lifeline that it was.

Come on, you've done this before, he thought. That was strictly accurate but it was only once in Alice's test area. And it was on a wall that was only ten feet high instead of this deathtrap. Still it was enough that he understood the principle.

He remembered the instructor Alice had set up for him telling him never to look down.

He looked between his feet and couldn't believe the drop. It was colossal.

Time to go man, Imaginary-Bobby said.

Jack gingerly moved his foot down a single step and felt the line take his weight. When it didn't snap and send him plunging to his death he risked another single step.

He was completely out of the window now, leaning back into a sitting position like the instructor had shown him, with his feet pressed as hard as he could into the wall. Beneath him was nothing but air.

It's working, he thought. He put one foot after the other they way the instructor had shown him and prayed that it would keep working.

It took Jack a moment or two to find a good rhythm but before long he'd got the hang of it and felt he was moving quite quickly. He risked another look down.

He'd gone about a third of the way.

He had no idea if that was good or bad because he'd lost all track of time so he fixed his eyes on the window above him and just kept moving.

He was just beginning to feel good about the whole thing and think he might have a chance to stop Abi when the smoke pouring from the window started to slow down to a trickle.

He knew what that meant. The fish tank had stopped producing steam. All the water was gone, the fish were dead, and when the room cleared and the doorman realised he was gone, he might join them.

It took another two minutes before the doorman's head appeared at the window. Jack was about halfway down the building. He'd have been quite pleased if it wasn't for the little voice that told him that meant he was halfway *up* the side of a building as well and a man intent on stopping him was above him looking down.

"You are not to leave," came the robotic voice from above.

Not very imaginative is he? Imaginary-Bobby said.

No. Any ideas what to do or are you just going to make smart-arse remarks?

Don't ask me. I'm just a part of you. If you haven't got any ideas then I haven't got any ideas.

Oh good. Thanks.

The doorman disappeared for a minute and Jack wondered where he had gone until the cord lurched in his hands and he fell down about three feet in one go.

"Argh!"

The cord went taut again and his back wrenched from the sudden stop.

The doorman's head reappeared. Jack couldn't make out his expression at this height but he guessed he wasn't happy.

He started trying to move faster but abseiling isn't designed for speed unless you're in the SAS. He thought of the films he'd seen where the hero jumped off a building and a rope gently lowered him down to the ground. If that was real why hadn't the bloody instructor showed him how to do that?!

"You are not to leave."

Jack kept lowering himself as fast as he could but had an idea.

"Wait, I'm coming back in!" Jack called up. He hoped the doorman's Shark-confused brain wouldn't be able to handle it and it would buy him some more time.

He was wrong.

If the doorman heard him he made no sign, he was still looking down towards Jack and he started doing something. Jack couldn't see what it was but he could see his arms moving.

What's he doing? Jack wondered.

Then, all at once, he found out. In the worst way possible.

One side of the looped cord came away from the wall. It felt down past him, narrowly missing his shoulder, and it plummeted to the ground below him. As he watched it go Jack realised what was happening. The doorman was cutting the cord. And he was half finished.

He barely had time to register what was going on before the other half came loose in his hands.

He seemed to hang in mid air for a split second before gravity kicked in.

Then he fell backwards like a stone towards the concrete below.

CHAPTER TWENTY

He was falling.

That was all that Jack's brain could process.

Wing suit! Wing suit! Imaginary-Bobby shouted in his head.

A part of Jack knew that it was his own subconscious using Bobby's voice but at that moment he could have kissed his brother.

There was no time at all to get himself into the right position so he didn't even bother trying.

As he hurtled towards the concrete, he pulled the sides of his tracksuit and they unfurled with a WHOOMPH!

The rushing air caught under them and for the second time in a minute Jack's body was felt as though it had been thumped by a giant.

He angled himself into the closest thing he could manage to a dive to reduce the impact. His fall started to slow but there wasn't time for the suit to work properly.

The suit slowed his fall but it couldn't actually give him any upwards lift. And it wasn't going to stop the pain.

He made it past the car park onto the grassed area and then, less than twenty seconds after the rope was cut, he crashed into the ground.

By that time he was moving more horizontally than vertically. Just about.

He tumbled head over heels, crashing without any elegance whatsoever. Brazilian Jiu-Jitsu didn't focus as much on *ukemi*, or how to break a fall properly, as the Japanese version did but it included the essentials and he had been taught them all. He managed none of it. He bounced more than rolled but, eventually, he came to a stop.

He turned himself over, painfully, and looked back up at the window. The doorman had disappeared again. Only the faint wisps of smoke still trailing from the window told him which one it was at all.

He didn't know if the doorman would have enough sense to get in touch with Abi if he failed but he had to assume that he would. That meant Jack had to move fast.

He tried gingerly to raise himself. Everything hurt but it was excruciating to stand up. His left leg in particular made him nearly scream each time he put it to the floor. He could just about support himself so he guessed he'd broken his ankle not his leg.

He stumbled his way across the concrete trying not to cry as he went.

He had to get to the launch.

Inside the main GamesCon hall he pushed his way past other people. He had expected to be stopped, but the place was full of people dressed up as characters from games. With his tracksuit trailing the extra material of the wings, no shoes and a face covered in grazes and grass stains, they all assumed he was just another fan in costume.

Yeah, Jack thought when the fourth person looked quizzically at him but didn't offer any help. *I'm from 'Fell from the Penthouse 3'. It's great. Little too realistic for my liking. Get out of the bloody way!*

Despite the funny looks it wasn't long before he got to the edge of the VIP area at front of the hall. It was roped off and there were two security guards on each side to keep out people who shouldn't be there.

Jack hovered on the outside and scanned the rows of people quickly.

The area was arranged into different sections depending on how 'V' important a person the GamesCon organisers thought you were. The beta testers and Elites all counted as VIPs, so too did the media, whether new internet media or traditional news outlets. But then there was the capital 'V' VIP area where the politicians and rich people were. That was where Sebastien's mother would have been standing... if she hadn't already been invited up on to the stage!

Standing either side of her were Simon Morton and Sauer. They were saying something, but between the roar of the crowd and the very loud music it was impossible to hear what it was.

He couldn't see Abi anywhere but she must be around here somewhere. Probably behind the stage ready for a quick getaway if necessary. He was really looking for Sebastien but he couldn't see him either.

He needed to get inside and look along every row. He must only have minutes. He didn't know how long they would keep the president up there talking but he didn't think it would be very long. No one really came to these things to see politicians.

He avoided the security guards' eyes and tried to walk through as though he belonged, in what he now thought of as the 'Wallace technique'. This time it didn't work.

"You can't go in there I'm afraid," the closest guard said.

"I need to see someone. I'm one of the beta testers."

They looked him up and down and Jack kept the pain off his face long enough for them to come to the same conclusion as everybody else, just a crazy fan in a costume. But they weren't going to let him in.

"Can I see your pass then?"

"I don't have it, it's in my room."

"You'll need to go and get it then, sorry."

Then he caught sight of Veteran and a couple of other Red Team members. They waved and gave him the same puzzled "What have you come as?" look. Finally standing next to them he saw Sandra and nearly cried out with relief. She'd be able to get him in.

"Sandra!" he called, his voice cracking from the pain.

She turned and looked around then spotted him. She hurried over.

"Hey Jack, how come you're not... Whoah! What happened to you?!"

"Costume. I'll tell you what it is when I'm inside. Can you tell these guys to let me in?"

Sandra smiled at the security men.

"Yeah, he's one of mine. He's alright."

"I understand that, Miss Coates, but without his pass we can't let him in."

"Can't you make an exception just this once?"

"Yesterday we could have but not today." The second security man flicked his head towards the row of official looking French security with guns and rolled his eyes at Sandra.

"Run upstairs and get it Jack. It won't take a minute," Sandra said.

"Yeah come back to us lad and we'll let you straight in," the first security guard said trying to be helpful.

Jack hardly heard him, over the man's shoulder he had seen one of the testers stand up.

It was Sebastien.

He was standing stock still like the doorman upstairs. He must be about to make his move.

"I need to get in there now!" Jack said and tried pushing past the men.

Sandra stepped back in alarm.

"Jack, what are you doing?" she said, sounding shocked.

The security guard was caught unawares by Jack's sudden move and for the tiniest of moments Jack thought he'd get past but as soon as he put his left foot down he cried out in pain and the man reached forward and grabbed him up in a bear hug.

Jack stamped down with his good foot and grazed the man's shin.

"You little!..."

The man cried out more in annoyance than real pain. Jack still had no shoes on and the man was wearing thick combat trousers as part of his uniform. But it was enough to unbalance him and the pair of them went down.

"Sebastien!" Jack shouted as he disappeared beneath the big guard.

Hearing his name broke through whatever hold Shark had on the French boy and his head turned in Jack's direction, but Jack was out of sight by the time he turned around. He looked momentarily confused but a second later his programming kicked back in and the look on his face was replaced by the vacant look the Elites all wore.

Jack watched from under the guard's meaty arm as Sebastien started moving towards the end of the aisle. There was no urgency to the boy's movements but this had to be it. He was really going to kill his own mum.

"No! Sebastien don't!" he shouted.

"Jack what the hell is going on?" Sandra asked.

Then the second guard reached down and pulled Jack from under the first one.

"Right that's enough of that. I don't know who you want in there but it isn't happening kid. Now knock it off or you're going to get properly hurt."

He held Jack with one big hand while he offered the other to his colleague and pulled him up, grinning.

"Knocked down by a kid, Paul. Nice one!"

Jack was close to despair. He'd come this far only to have to watch while Sebastien carried out Abi's horrible plan. And his rescue attempt was so pathetic that the security guards were joking with each other about it.

He didn't know what to do.

Behind the guards Sandra was saying something to him but he couldn't listen to her, he could only watch as Sebastien got closer.

His route out of the crowd brought him towards Jack and Jack could see the blue glow from his glasses. He wanted to cry from the pain and the sense of failure.

The thought flashed through his mind to ask Sandra to help but there was no way that would work now, she thought he was mad. He looked at her, he had never seen her lose her cool since the first time he met her. Something about the way her head was angled triggered a completely unrelated memory of the time she had demonstrated Shark to him for the first time, flicking her Shark generated green hair side to side.

Suddenly he knew what he had to do.

Maybe there was no way to stop Sebastien killing the president but he *could* use Shark to change who he thought the president was. Jack fumbled in his pocket, still ignoring Sandra's shouts and the guards mocking each other, and pulled out Abi's tablet.

Sandra's pitch rose and he guessed she was asking where he'd got the tablet from but he concentrated on the screen.

He'd seen her do this. If he could just find the... there it was.

He clicked on the reference to Sebastien's glasses and got access to their reality filters. Now he needed another set to be the target. Sandra was the closest person with a Shark ID to him so he selected her and his fingers flew over the tablet as he programmed Sebastien's glasses to see Sandra's Shark ID as his mum.

At the same time he leant forward and grabbed Sandra's glasses off her face and shoved them onto his own, calling out again to get the French boy's attention.

"Sebastien! Over here!"

"Now, that's it sonny," the first guard said, all humour now gone from his voice. "I don't know what your problem is but I've had enough of you."

Sebastien came to a stop at the end of the aisle. He had heard his name being called and this time it had seemed to come from his mother.

In the world that his glasses showed him there were two French presidents, two mothers, two targets. He had to kill them both.

But one was closer.

He rushed at Jack.

Oblivious to the boy hurtling towards his back, the guard was still shouting and making a grab at Jack as Jack, ignoring the agony from his ankle, was weaving about trying to keep out of his reach while at the same time staying visible to Sebastien.

"Give them back to Miss Coates and you're coming with me..." the guard said right as Sebastien crashed into him.

Sebastien was bigger than Jack and the guard hadn't been expecting it. He went over onto the floor face down, Sebastien landing on top of him and knocking the air from him.

Before the other guard could react, Sebastien scrambled off the first guard's back and grabbed hold of Jack by the throat with both hands and started squeezing.

Despite the pain he was in, Jack's jiu-jitsu training kicked in and he reacted automatically. He landed one good punch in Sebastien's face and started to get him in a Garcia-style x-guard before he managed to stop himself. The point wasn't to win, it was to stop Abi.

He relaxed and just had time to wonder if the Director would honour his deal if he was dead. Then he lost consciousness.

When he woke up Agent Wallace was leaning over him. The battledroid costume was gone, replaced this time not by one of his fancy suits but by a black tactical vest with POLICE written all over it.

"What happened?" Jack asked.

"You fainted."

"Blacked out," Jack said.

"Pardon?"

"Never mind. I didn't mean what happened to me. I meant did I stop it?"

Wallace grinned.

"You did. Brilliant job, son. The commotion you kicked off disrupted the launch and the French security service bundled the president off the stage. I assume, given that your French friend over there is babbling about you being his mother, that she was the target?"

Jack struggled to sit up. Then became aware he was on some sort of ambulance stretcher. Wallace had cleared some space around him. Sebastien was handcuffed a little way away and did indeed seem to be babbling. Jack noted with a degree of satisfaction that he also had the beginnings of a black eye. He was surrounded by armed policemen but none of them were paying him any attention.

"How come you are here?" Jack asked Wallace.

"CIRCLE leave no spy behind, Jack. I figured that whatever was going to happen would probably happen on the launch day so I moved the team in closer. We were in the crowd but we didn't see anything unusual until he attacked you."

"Nothing unusual? I half-abseiled, half-flew down the side of a building then stormed through the crowd while wearing a parachute suit and no shoes, and you didn't spot anything unusual. Have you ever thought you might be in the wrong business, Wallace?"

Just then there was a bustle of activity and a group of armed men pushed their way through the crowd and headed for Sebastien. Jack judged by the acronym on their jackets that these were the French security people.

Heated words were exchanged between the British police and the French security service but after a moment the French group parted to reveal the president. The police stood aside and the security team undid Sebastien's handcuffs and helped him to his feet. They closed ranks around Sebastien and his mother again and started moving away.

As they passed Jack's stretcher, Sebastien raised a hand and the little parade stopped.

Jack smiled up at Sebastien and waited for him to say something. Sebastien looked down at him and shook his head in an attempt at disgust. His swollen right eye somewhat undermined the effect.

"I told you I would kick your ass in a fight," he said and then waved imperiously at his guard and they all started moving again.

Jack was speechless. The French prat wasn't joking at all. Jack knew some people were just plain jerks and he didn't particularly want to make friends with Sebastien, but he had expected him to be at least slightly grateful for the fact that he'd saved him from killing his mother. Abi had been right. The boy was a first class idiot.

That reminded him, what had happened to Abi? He looked for Wallace to ask him but he was off talking to one of the policemen. He lay back on his stretcher and started to close his eyes but was interrupted by another French accent.

He opened his eyes and saw that the little French parade had stopped once more and the guards had opened up to surround Jack and the president.

Well, at least she's grateful, he thought and struggled to sit up again.

"Madame President, I am glad you are okay," he said in his best French.

The president's eyebrows raised very slightly, no doubt surprised by his knowledge of French but she contained her reaction and switched to English.

"You have already hurt my son's face, Monsieur Dawson, please do not do the same to my country's language," she said with a snooty air. "I have stopped only to say that you may think you have done something good here today, but Sebastien is not like you... normal boys. He is being prepared for a career in politics. If you really wish to help your friend you will keep silent about this."

And then, with a more polished version of Sebastien's imperious wave to get her people moving, she was gone leaving Jack bewildered as to how someone could say so little but get so much of it wrong.

What a cow! Like mother, like bloody son, he thought. Jack wouldn't get a vote in the French elections because he was too young. And not French. But if he did he knew he wouldn't vote for her.

He lay back and closed his eyes properly this time. He'd had enough of the spy game.

CHAPTER TWENTY ONE

Jack didn't see Wallace again for another week.

He was pretty sure that the ambulance he had eventually been rolled into was a CIRCLE front and the nurse who had been with him the whole time he spent in the hospital was almost definitely a CIRCLE agent. But the hospital itself seemed real enough and they had checked him in under the name of Jack Dawson so he had stuck to his cover story.

The hospital kept him in for a couple of days while they ran tests that seemed to keep failing for some reason. He guessed that the nurse was doing something to delay things and CIRCLE just wanted him to have some time to recover. Why no-one could tell him that, though, escaped him. It seemed like secrecy was a habit for CIRCLE.

Eventually the nurse disappeared and the hospital discharged him on a pair of crutches. A car was waiting outside to take him back to the foster home. He didn't want to go but he didn't have a lot of choice in the matter. The driver told him Wallace would be in touch and gave him a letter for the home that explained he had been held in witness protection while he helped a department of the government that dealt with gang crime.

Jack didn't think they'd buy it but they did. They probably didn't care enough to challenge it.

He went back to school on the Wednesday. It was weird not being able to tell anyone about it but he didn't think it was a good idea to trust any of his mates with it. Not that they'd believe him anyway.

He spent the evenings at Frank's phone shop as normal and fell back into playing SWAT Team IV. He had to claw back some of his ranking because that much time away meant he'd fallen in the league.

He'd been afraid Frank would challenge him about being at GamesCon, but although he talked excitedly about what a weird convention it had been with Shark being almost released and then pulled, he hadn't seen Jack. Jack couldn't understand that until he remembered that, to the audience, the game had made him look like the terrorist.

And CIRCLE, or maybe Sebastien's mum, had hushed up any notion of an attack on the French President.

In short, life pretty much got back to normal. Even if the inside of his head didn't.

Saturday rolled around and Jack was able to go and see Bobby again.

He'd made the appointment as soon as he knew he was being discharged from the hospital, but the earliest he could see him was today. He left the home early in the morning and headed for the bus stop that would start the long journey to Bobby's remand centre.

A car pulled up alongside him as he swung along on his crutches and gave him a shock when the driver called his name.

"Give you a lift, Jack?"

Jack bent and looked through the open passenger window. It was Wallace. Jack was excited to see him but he didn't want him to know that so he hid his reaction.

"I'm going to see Bobby."

"We know, but I was hoping you could spare me some time. I can drop you at the prison when we're done."

Jack hobbled to the passenger side, stuck his crutches onto the floor in the back and got in the front next to Wallace.

Wallace glanced across at him.

"Good to see you again, Jack. How's the ankle?" he said as he pulled out into the traffic.

"It hurts. Remind me to lodge a complaint you can pass to Alice about her wingsuit."

Wallace chuckled. "I don't think she's big on critical feedback. But you can always give it a go yourself. That's where we're going now."

"No blindfold?"

Wallace smiled.

"Not this time Jack. Though you will have to sign the Official Secrets Act."

Wallace drove on in silence. Finally they pulled up in a normal suburban side road outside a small park. Jack could see kids playing in the park beyond the metal fence and wondered if Wallace had brought him for a talk where they couldn't be overheard before they went to HQ.

"This is us," Wallace said, getting out of the car.

Jack did the same and then stood there confused as Wallace immediately got into the back seat of the car. Wallace leant over to his side, pushed open the door and gestured for Jack to get in.

"You might want to hold onto your crutches," he said as Jack got in. "And buckle up."

He reached behind himself as he spoke and secured his seatbelt with a clunk. Jack frowned but picked up his crutches as he had been asked and laid them across his and Wallace's laps. Then he put his own belt on and sat there looking straight ahead.

He felt stupid, the two of them sitting in the back seat with their seatbelts on.

"What are we doing?" he asked.

"You'll see."

Wallace pulled his phone out and punched a combination of digits that Jack didn't see. A couple of seconds later he jumped as the seat started sinking.

It made him jump and Wallace laughed.

"What is it with you people and your secret entrances?!" he asked, laughing as well.

"This is one of my favourites," Wallace confided with a wink.

The seat descended slowly for a moment and Jack saw something slide into place across the opening they had left above them. He couldn't tell what it was from underneath but he guessed from the outside of the car it looked like another seat.

The light disappeared as the new seat slid into place and Jack and Wallace were left in the dark.

"Hold tight to those crutches," Wallace said.

"Wh?...Aaaaaargh!"Jack started to ask but it was lost in a scream as the bottom of the seat made contact with something underneath and then rocketed forward. He grabbed the crutches more by reflex than choice.

The seat shot them along at a speed that felt like the fastest Jack had ever travelled. It wouldn't have been quite right to call it a rollercoaster because it was mostly straight, but the adrenaline rush was the same. A handful of times they went over a small hill or round a gentle bend but they never slowed, and each time Jack felt like he'd left his stomach behind.

It was amazing.

Eventually they shot out of the darkness into an area with lights and came to a stop. Jack couldn't help himself, he turned to Wallace and breathlessly asked, "Can we do that again?!"

"Well, we've got to get back at the end, haven't we?" he said with a twinkle in his eye. "I told you it was my favourite. Come on, the Director is expecting us."

Wallace stepped off the car seat onto a wooden platform and opened the only door. Beyond it Jack could see a lift that he recognised from the last time he had come to CIRCLE HQ.

He clambered awkwardly out of the seat, settled his crutches under his arm and limped after Wallace. Once he was inside Wallace spoke to the artificially intelligent computer system that ran HQ and the lift started to move. It stopped much quicker than it had on his last visit and someone with a lab coat got in.

"Hawke!" Jack raised his head and saw Alice's purple hair on top of a face that was smiling for the first time. "I hear you did a really good job out there. Nice one!"

"Thanks Alice," he said. Jack was thrilled that she thought he'd done well.

The lift started again and Alice turned away.

"Didn't you have something you were going to say to Alice, Jack?" Wallace asked innocently.

Jack looked at him in horror but there was no sign on his face of the amusement he must be feeling. Alice looked back at him over her shoulder.

"Yeah, what was that?"

Jack swallowed. "Just... You know, thanks for the kit. It was really useful."

"No problem kid. Stop by another time and we'll see what we can sort out for you," Alice said as the lift came to a halt and the doors opened.

Jack thought it was an odd thing to say but he was so relieved he just smiled at her.

"See you later Alice," Wallace called as the doors closed behind her.

"What was that for?" Jack hissed at him.

Wallace shrugged

"I thought it would be funny. You've so obviously got a crush on her."

"I have not!" Jack protested.

"If you say so," Wallace said and turned to face the front again.

Jack looked sideways at Wallace. *He's alright,* he thought. *More like a mate than anything.*

The rest of the journey was uneventful and before long they'd arrived outside the Director's office. The Director must have been notified by the AI that they had arrived because she spoke to Wallace through the intercom as soon as they walked up to the door.

"One minute Agent, I am just finishing something off."

Wallace and Jack went and stood by the railing and Jack bent his head as far as he dared over the railing to look down into the pit. He could see the Weapons test area below and make out some people busying around two cars but there didn't seem to be anything interesting at this distance.

After a minute he heard the door to the Director's office swing open and a man hurried out looking very annoyed. Jack recognised him from the news.

The man hurried off down the corridor accompanied by an agent who had been waiting for him discreetly.

"Wasn't that..." Jack began but Wallace shook his head quickly at him.

"We don't discuss visitors to HQ, Jack."

"Oh. Right."

"Come in gentlemen!" the Director called from inside her room.

Wallace gave Jack a little nod and Jack started to head in, but Wallace held his arm back for a second.

"Just be yourself and keep your cool. You have fans here, Jack," he said quietly, then let go of Jack's arm and strode into the room.

Jack followed him, puzzled by what he'd said but trying to remember his earlier advice about looking confident. He didn't think he had the stride quite right.

"Mr Hawke," the Director said. She seemed genuinely pleased to see him.

"Mrs er... Director," Jack replied.

"Just Director is fine. Take a seat both of you." Wallace did so Jack copied him. His seat was still warm from the man he had seen leaving.

I'm sitting in a chair the Prime Minister has just used, Jack thought. *That's mental.*

"Well, Jack I've called you in to say well done and formally close down this operation," she gestured at the screen of her expensive desktop computer. Jack couldn't see it but assumed there was some sort of file open on there. She glanced quickly at the screen and then at a paper notepad in front of her before looking up at Jack and continuing, "It has all had a very satisfactory end. You will have seen from the news during your brief hospital stay that the company decided not to launch Shark. However, unless you read the financial papers you may not have noticed that that seems to have caused a downward spiral in Morton Tech's share price. It has rather unfortunately collapsed and the company is now being closed down. A nice piece of stock market work that last bit Wallace," she smiled at Wallace.

"Thank you Director. I had to call in some favours from the Ministry of Defence computer team but it's done the trick."

"Indeed." She swivelled her chair to look back at Jack and continued bringing him up to date. "Dr Sauer has vanished without trace. And I'm sure you'll have heard that Simon Morton was overcome by the spectacular failure of Shark and sadly killed himself in despair."

Jack shifted in his chair and fought the urge to raise his hand. The Director noticed and paused to let him speak.

"That isn't real is it? It was all over the news but I didn't believe it."

The Director glanced across and nodded minutely at Wallace. Jack followed her eyes and it was the agent who answered.

"I'm afraid Sauer really has got away but no Jack, you're right about Morton. We have him in a secure holding facility. We would like to understand Shark a bit better and he is... helping us with our enquiries."

"What about Abi? His daughter, I mean."

"No one knows where she is. She appears to have run away. I say good luck to her if she can make a new life for herself out of the shadow of her father's crimes."

"You need to find her." Both the Director and Wallace seemed taken aback. "It was her. I thought you knew that when you sent me that message?"

Wallace looked confused. "No. We just wanted to make sure you didn't share anything with her that would jeopardise the mission if she told her father. You're not really saying it was her?"

"Yes. Really. She was behind the whole thing."

"She's just a kid, Jack," Wallace said, incredulously.

"I'd have thought you'd have realised by now, there's no such thing as *just* a kid," Jack said, annoyed that, despite everything he'd been through, they were still underestimating anyone under the age of eighteen.

The Director coughed slightly and drew their attention back to her.

"This can keep for now Jack, I have a tight schedule. Wallace will debrief you afterwards and determine if there needs to be any course of action for the girl. For now though there is one other matter we need to discuss."

Jack could tell she didn't believe him about Abi but he dropped it for now. He'd just have to get Wallace on side afterwards. Her 'one other matter' must be about when they were getting Bobby out. He smiled and turned fully in his chair to face her and waited for her to explain but what she said next surprised him.

"You've proven yourself quite capable and we, I, would like to know if you would like to work with us again in the future. We may well have need for somebody who can get in to places our normal operatives can't. Would you be interested in that?"

Jack was flattered but he hadn't forgotten why he started working with them in the first place. This woman had sat in this very office and blackmailed him.

"I... I don't know. I only worked with you to protect Bobby. I'd need to check with him when he gets out. I don't know whether he'll want to move away or what." The woman clasped her hands together on the desk and out of the corner of his eye he saw Wallace cross and recross his legs uncomfortably. He got a sinking feeling. "Now that I've done what you wanted you're going to release him, right?"

The friendly mask dropped from the Director's face instantly and Jack saw the cold, power wielding woman he remembered from his first visit.

"You have to understand that it isn't quite as simple as all that Jack."

Jack's face darkened.

"You told me it was."

"Well, I said we'd do what we could," she said, her tone of voice extremely level and reasonable.

"No. You told me you'd get him released."

"Well, if I said that..."

"You did," Jack interrupted.

Wallace leant across and laid a calming hand on the side of his arm. Jack didn't look at him. He kept staring straight at the Director.

"*If* I said that," she repeated, her voice like ice now. "Then I mis-spoke. But CIRCLE does everything it can to protect its own and we see you as one of our own." She paused and gave Jack her most piercing look. It felt like she was looking into his soul. "You are one of ours aren't you, Jack?"

Jack sat in silence. He'd heard that it was a good negotiating tactic, but in truth he was silent because he didn't trust himself to speak without shouting and swearing. He was pretty sure that wouldn't help him or Bobby.

The Director took his silence as agreement and continued, once again sounding completely reasonable.

"So we will do what we can. But it might take a little longer than I'd like to get him cleared altogether. We have, however, been able to get him transferred to a more convenient location for you and we've arranged for you to be able to visit him every day. CIRCLE will also provide a lawyer. I'm sure it will be resolved quicker than for most people who find themselves in his situation." She spread her hands, palms up and when she brought them together again it was as though the matter was closed. She moved back to what she considered the important point. "In the meantime we'd like you to stay on our books as an agent in training."

Jack understood the subtext here well enough. He wasn't really being given a choice. Or not a choice he was prepared to make, at any rate.

"Okay."

"Okay? That's great. Agent Wallace will take you from here and get you processed and we'll be in touch to arrange your training."

"Or when you get news on Bobby."

"Oh yes, of course, or then."

She looked down at her desk, moved a sheet of paper to the centre and picked up her pen. Wallace stood and Jack realised they'd been dismissed. He got to the door before she spoke again.

"You really did do a good job Jack. You're one I'll be watching."

Jack didn't reply.

After they left the Director's office, Wallace and Jack had gone all the way back to the car in silence. Even the rollercoaster didn't make them speak.

Only once they'd got into the car did Wallace finally speak.

"I'm sorry about that Jack."

"You knew. While you were pretending to be my friend and mucking about in the lift. You knew."

"I didn't. I promise you. But I did expect something similar. You've got to understand Jack, she has to protect the country and she does everything she thinks is necessary to do that."

"Like lying to children and keeping my brother in jail."

Wallace sighed gently.

"She didn't put him in jail in the first place Jack. Remember that. She's just using what's available to her. And if you're going to hate anyone then hate me. I found you."

Jack didn't know what to say to that. After a minute Wallace spoke again.

"I'll be in touch to arrange a debriefing about the girl. In the meantime CIRCLE really have sorted out daily access for you at Bobby's. Do you want me to drop you there?"

He said 'Bobby's' like it was a flat. He didn't say 'prison'.

Jack was tempted to refuse but it would have been childish. Besides, as much as he hated her for it, and he did, Wallace was right about the Director. And he couldn't hate Wallace himself. He was clearly a good man.

"Yes please," he said simply.

Wallace nodded, put the car into gear and pulled away from the kerb.

CHAPTER TWENTY TWO

That night Jack was round at Frank's again playing SWAT Team IV. It wasn't going very well, his head wasn't really in the game but he was desperate to get back to normality.

He'd just finished a game against some diamond level players in which he'd got well and truly smashed and was trying to decide whether to call it a night, when he got a request for a voice message from a new user.

He would normally dismiss these sorts of messages as they tended to be wannabes trying to get onto a team, but he sat up straighter in his chair when he saw the username.

> Voice message request from: SharkGirl!

He accepted the call and spoke into his headset mic.

"Log-ons to SWAT Team IV can be traced you know," he said instead of hello.

"Not the way I do them, they can't," Abi replied. "I'm surprised to find you're still playing these things. Haven't you had enough of video games?"

"You wrecked my summer, Abi, and my trust in girls who won't give me their surname. You're not wrecking gaming for me as well. What do you want?"

"Maybe I just wanted to chat?"

"I expect you have other people you can chat to."

"Yeah, but you know what the normal people are like. So boring. I'm glad I didn't kill you. I enjoyed our time together."

Jack knew that despite everything he'd enjoyed her company too. And he knew she knew that. But that didn't mean they could still be friends.

"Is Sauer with you, Abi? I heard he got away."

Abi hesitated slightly before answering as though it bothered her what Jack thought. "I know how you feel about him Jack, and you're right, but he can be useful. I've got him under tighter control now, he won't do anything at all unless I let him."

"Yeah, I'm sure." Jack sighed. "Abi, why are you calling me? Seriously."

"I've had time to think about something you said in my dad's suite."

"What was that?" Jack asked, casting his mind back.

"About me asking you to join me."

Jack was grateful the call was voice only because he wasn't able to stop his eyebrows shooting up when she said it.

She can't be serious, he thought.

"Join you in what?" he asked.

"I've looked into your past, Jack Hawke." She heard his sharp intake of breath and answered the question he didn't ask. "Yes, I found out who you really are. It wasn't hard once I knew to start looking. I should have done it before but... something stopped me. I don't know why."

All at once Jack understood. He knew why she hadn't looked into him before when it had been so easy to do it even while she was on the run. He remembered the time in the corridor outside his room after Sebastien had shown that video and her reaction when he thought she had made Sebastien do all those cruel things to him. She liked him. The evil-genius girl was calling him because she liked him. He'd never had a girlfriend, never wanted one. He wasn't exactly opposed to the idea and he knew under different circumstances he could have liked Abi. *Damn, I know I did like her,* he thought honestly. But this was ridiculous. He wasn't about to hook up with someone who had done what she had.

Abi, unaware that he had worked out what was making her call, was still talking.

"... And I know about your brother. I could help. We could get him out Jack. We're smarter than they are."

"Abi, I'm not going to join you," he said, cutting her off. "Maybe I have done some dodgy things. Okay, there's no maybe about it, I have done some dodgy things, but you're some sort of criminal mastermind. The things I did were to help me and Bobby survive. You're just doing this for fun. And people are dying, Abi."

He had tried to keep his voice calm, trying not to upset the murderous criminal, but it hadn't worked. By the end it was obvious he was disgusted with her. He heard her take a breath while she worked out what to do now. She had expected him to agree.

She came out fighting.

"You don't want to make an enemy of me, Jack."

"I don't want to make an enemy of anyone, Abi. I never have. Turn yourself in."

"Why would I do that? The beta version of Shark was released, Jack. To lots of people. You and your friends might have stopped the main launch so it didn't get into every home and school like I wanted, but there are still lots and lots of people out there I can control. You haven't heard the last of me."

"Abi..." Jack said but his headset was silent.

She had gone and Jack was alone. He took off his headset and shut down the game.

So this was his new life as a spy, clandestine night time calls from super-criminals.

It was going to take a bit of getting used to.

~~THE END~~

Jack Hawke will return very soon in...
GENERAL MAYHEM

JOIN THE **JACK HAWKE FAN CLUB** AND BE ONE OF THE FIRST TO HEAR WHEN A NEW **JACK HAWKE** BOOK IS RELEASED

Sign up now and get a FREE copy of the 12 page reports that *TOP SECRET* spy agency CIRCLE pulled together on their newest teenage spy.

I promise I'll never spam you, but you'll get things like: behind the scenes information on Jack, exclusive free stories, updates, book release details and more. I will never pass on your email address and you can opt-out at any time.

YOU CAN SIGN UP AT
www.sannox.org.uk/jack-hawke-sign-up/

A NOTE FROM THE AUTHOR

Killer Game is my first published book for younger readers. I hope you enjoyed reading it as much as I enjoyed writing it! Why not drop me an email at contactus@sannox.org.uk and let me know what you think? I love hearing from readers and I read all of my email myself (and try to reply to it as far as possible).

Can I ask you to do something?

If you enjoyed *Killer Game* would you go and leave a quick review now for me? It will take less than five minutes but it really helps independent authors like me.

And if you just want to let me know you've done that or get in touch for any other reason then you can use the email address above.

If you want to keep up to date with my writing then the best way is to join all of the other readers on my mailing list by signing up at http://eepurl.com/dMMbwA. I won't bombard you with emails (I'm too busy writing!) but you'll get to find out about my upcoming books before anyone else. I always run a "welcome aboard" offer of some free reading material and I often use the list to offer pre-release copies of new material for review so you'll be even further ahead of the crowd.

And finally, some "thank you"s

I've been writing long enough now that I've collected a small group of people who read early drafts for me and help catch typos or embarrassing moments. Being listed in every book has no doubt lost its appeal for them now, but you know who you are and I hope you know that I just as grateful now as I was the first time.

However, there were two new members of the "team" (not sure you can be a team if you've never met and each of you only interacts with me!) that I would particularly like to thank for their input to Killer Game:

Andy Hall for taking the time to read something outside of his usual genre and still offering helpful comments; and

Andy Nicholl who earns extra marks for spotting a typo in my single line of French as well as the usual number in my English!

Thank you both very much, and welcome to the "team"!

Michael Lancashire
2018

ABOUT THE AUTHOR

Michael Lancashire has written a series of books for adults about the Architect, a criminal mastermind. *Killer Game* is the first in his new series of Jack Hawke books.
He (Michael, not Jack) lives with his wife, three kids, and an ever changing assortment of chickens, mammals and reptiles. They split their time between the Midlands and a Scottish island that's remaining unnamed for now.

The books featuring the Architect are:
The Voynich Deception
Kernel Panic
The Keycode: An Architect Short Story
The Fourth Target
Almost Out
Trapped

He has also written a British political thriller:
Heritage: A short story

Links to all of the above at your favourite store are available on his website sannox.org.uk

21517746R00120

Printed in Great Britain
by Amazon